A NEW ME

———————— ❧ ————————

Carlos Must Go!

T A M E K A   S O N O M A

authorHOUSE®

AuthorHouse™
1663 Liberty Drive
Bloomington, IN 47403
www.authorhouse.com
Phone: 1 (800) 839-8640

Published by AuthorHouse   12/01/2016

ISBN: 978-1-5246-5269-2 (sc)
ISBN: 978-1-5246-5268-5 (e)

Library of Congress Control Number: 2016919882

Print information available on the last page.

Any people depicted in stock imagery provided by Thinkstock are
models, and such images are being used for illustrative purposes only.
Certain stock imagery © Thinkstock.

This book is printed on acid-free paper.

C H A P T E R

A Love That Lied

Was it me? Was it him? Why did he do that to me? Maybe I'm just not pretty enough. All I know is that he was wrong for treating me that way. Well, it's his loss anyhow.

My name is Denita Camacho, and I'm a student at Morris A. Bachelor High School. My parents moved us here to Chicago to pursue better jobs and find a school where I would be happy. Happy? Not so much at first.

My new school is cool, especially the guys! Let's talk about this one guy who is so fine that he made me feel like yelling at the top of my lungs, "He is so gorgeous!" Every time I looked at him, I wanted to tell him that I loved him. But as it turned out, he definitely didn't feel the same about me. He was always lying about something crazy. It's been two years since my ex-boyfriend and I broke up. He never treated me like I was special or his one and only. That loser! That son of a—

Oh, wait! Did I tell you the fool's name? It's Carlos Lugo. You need to know a little's fine background before I get into the twisted romance that never should have been.

The summer when I was fifteen years old, my parents decided that they needed to make more money for the family. (I thought that what we had before was fine, but they always seem to want more.) So that was the reason we moved from

Portland to Chicago. Personally, I missed Oregon. All my friends were still there. I especially loved hanging out with my best friend, Alan Shrivadello. We met in the first grade, and we were always together. Alan never lied to me, and I was always honest with him. Even after I moved, we remained close, and we still are.

My dad decided to use the family's van to move to Chicago. My mother thought we should rent a J-Haul truck, but Dad thought that using the van would be cheaper. How annoying! During the move, they argued about how Dad never listened to Mom and how he never paid attention to spending. On and on, back and forth—that was our long trip on the road. I'm surprised that I didn't need Tylenol or something. The whole trip took thirty-four hours. Ridiculous, I know. With parents like mine, even a one-day car trip can seem like fifteen years in a torture chamber, but they always seem to make up somewhere along the road. Maybe it's my mother's calming voice.

Anyway, those are my parents, Marcus and Rubia Camacho, straight from Brooklyn, New York.

When we arrived in Chicago, I felt like a new person. I felt so energized, and the city looked amazing! My parents had bought a cute little blue-and-white house with four bedrooms and two bathrooms, so there was plenty of room for all five of us.

Wow, I didn't mention my brother and sister. Anoki is eighteen and a senior at my high school. He thinks he's Michael Jordan, Shaq, and Carmelo Anthony wrapped into one body. Of course, he plays basketball very well, and the girls have always loved him. My parents never have to worry about Anoki, because he's always a gentleman with the girls. He is also very smart, so he'll have no problem doing whatever he wants to do. Orlana is twenty. She's an undergrad at Forester-Shane University. She received the Victoria Andrews Scholarship for good grades, so she's going to college for free. She has way too many talents to name, but here are a few: she dances, sings, paints, speaks fluent Spanish, and is an excellent cook. And did I mention that she's a black belt in karate? She is amazing, just like Anoki. It was easy for them to adjust to Chicago, because they're fantastic. I'm good with this city now, but I didn't really want to be here at first.

In school, I have met a few people I like hanging around with. First there is Luisa Vega. Luisa and I have become very close because we both love the rapper Drake. We met in the lunchroom when we were just sitting around talking, and since then she's become my best friend in this town. Her nickname for me is Morena—she says she loves my medium-brown complexion since she's so light-skinned. Mercedes Maldonado is another one my good friends. She loves to have fun. Unlike Luisa, she's always daring me do something crazy funny. She's another *Boricua*. One day she dared me to kiss a guy in my class and run away. Have you ever heard of such foolishness? Of course, I never did her dare. She figured I wouldn't do it anyway.

Now we can discuss Alicia Sigmorella. She is African American and Welsh. Isn't that weird? That is definitely an interesting mix. It's because of her that I've grown to love art since I've come to Chicago. The only problem I have with Alicia is that I'm not her. I'm just really glad that she's my friend. My parents believe she's a good influence on me, and I think they're right.

As a freshman, I got along with practically everyone in my school and neighborhood, but there was one girl I thought needed to lock herself in the closet and never come out. This thorn in my flesh was named Brenda Sampson. Brenda was a stupid white girl who lived with her head up her ass all day. Do you want to know why I despised this girl so much? Well, she was just so conceited and never stayed in her lane. One time I was in the gym, talking to a guy named James Delton. James was in my fifth-period math class, and since I sucked at math, he'd offered to tutor me. Brenda was walking by and said to him, "You might as well kiss your weekends good-bye if you're gonna tutor this one. Denita has no math skills whatsoever." James ignored her. Also he is gay, so she really needed to mind her own business. I should have snatched her fake eyelashes off her. Anyway, none of my friends seemed to like Brenda, and that was totally fine with me.

So you're probably wondering about my ex-boyfriend. In case you forgot, his name is Carlos Lugo. I hate to admit it, but Carlos is very cute. Actually, he is a Puerto Rican god! He can make any girl fall for him. He has that type of personality. When we first met, I was a freshman. I had just come to Morris A. Bachelor High School, and I really thought he was cute. Actually, that is how I met Mercedes. She introduced us. One day we were in the cafeteria during fourth-period lunch, and she noticed me looking at Carlos and asked me if I liked him. We didn't know his name at the time, so she went and asked him. I was so embarrassed, but Mercedes knew I was afraid to talk to him. She talked to him for a few minutes, and I could see her looking over at me. After she finished, she came back to tell me what they had talked about.

She said, "Girl, he is so fine and smells so good. I think he's wearing Armani Code. Anyway, his name is Carlos Lugo. He's Puerto Rican like us, and he thinks you're cute too. He wants to meet you. Denita, you should wait for him in the gym after school, because he has football practice. Maybe y'all can talk. You should definitely talk to him before Brenda sinks her fake nails into him."

I took Mercedes's advice and waited for Carlos in the gym after school. While I was watching him during football practice, all I kept thinking was *Look at him looking so fine! What am I going to say to him?* It was such a stressful moment for me. Here was this hot-lookin' dude that I liked, and I had no idea what to say to him. When he finally finished practice, I felt like falling out on the floor. I'm sure I had a blank look on my face the whole time he was walking toward me. I finally got my focus back when he shook my hand and said, "Hi. I'm Carlos Lugo. Thanks for waiting for me." All I could think was *Wow! He has the most amazing light-brown eyes.* He was taller than me, and looking up at him felt so romantic.

He wanted to talk, so we went to a nearby park to sit on a bench under the trees. We talked about school, our friends, and anything else that came to mind. Everything felt so right, especially when he said, "Denita, you are so cute. Do you have a boyfriend? I had a girlfriend, but we broke up."

I really had no idea what to say next. It took about five seconds for me to come up with "No." That's it! How was I supposed to know that this hot guy was going to ask me if I had a boyfriend?

Well, Carlos looked shocked when I told him that. He said, "You are way too cute to be alone. If I was your man, I would never let you go." Can you believe that he said that? I was in love for several hours after that.

By now it was about four o'clock, and my mother called me on my iPhone, wondering what was taking me so long to get home. I told her that I was with a friend in the park and was on my way. Of course, I normally would have called if I was going to be late, but I just lost track of time. Carlos seemed so worried for me—he asked if he could walk me home. (It turned out that he lived three blocks from my house.) As he was walking me home, he tried to hold my hand. My first reaction was to pull away. He stopped and said, "Okay, I didn't mean to scare you. I just like kicking it with you. You're so smart and beautiful that I couldn't resist. Please don't be mad." How could I have been mad at him for that? So I put my hand in his, and we strolled down the street. I was so lucky that my dad didn't know I was with a guy. He would have driven to get me and ruined that fabulous moment.

When Carlos walked me to my door, I felt like a lady. He was such a gentleman. When we said good-bye to each other, he actually kissed me on my forehead. Oh my goodness, his lips were so soft! My parents were in the living room when I came in the door. My father said, "How was school?" I was in such a daze that I don't even remember what I said to him. My mother might have said something, but who knows.

As soon as I got upstairs, my sister, Orlana, said to me with bright eyes, "Where were you? Were you with a boy? You know how Daddy is, so you shouldn't even tell him yet."

I must have had a confused look on my face. "I have no idea why Daddy would care, because I was with a friend."

My sister always knows when there is more to the story. "Is that friend a guy?" she asked, smiling.

At that point I gave in, because I knew she would find out anyway. "Yes, Orlana," I blurted out. "I was with a boy named Carlos. He goes to my high school. Are you happy now?"

Orlana couldn't stop smiling as we sat on my bed and I told her how cute he was. My sister was very perceptive about me and my happiness. She never harassed me about anything I did, because she knew that I always made the right decisions. She said, "Denita, I knew you were with a boy today because I could see it in your eyes. He sounds nice, but guys always show you the good side of them when you first meet them. Don't be fooled, girl." Orlana always gave good advice, so I listened very carefully to her.

After dinner, Luisa called me, sounding excited. "Girl! What happened today? Mercedes told me about a guy named Carlos that you like. Tell me all about it, Morena." Of course, I had to tell my close friend what was going on. Luisa was crazy, though. In her mind I was married to Carlos already, and he hadn't even met my family yet.

Anyway, it was a nice evening with Carlos. I have never forgotten that night.

Carlos and I became inseparable during our freshman year. If I wanted pizza, he came with me. If he wanted to see a movie, I always made sure that I was there with him. There was nothing that could have kept me apart from Carlos. Everyone seemed to know that we were a couple. The only thing that bothered me about our relationship was what my parents said to me after they met him.

My mother was probably the most open about her concerns. Anoki told our parents about Carlos' rude treatment toward females. She came to me in my room one day and said, "Honey, I don't trust that boy. He seems like he has a hidden agenda with you. Be careful with that one, and watch your back."

After she said that, I worried a little, but not too much. My father actually surprised me, though, since fathers are usually tougher in these situations. He just said very calmly, "I don't have to tell you to be careful, because I know you will be—you always do the right thing. But if Carlos hurts you, I'm done playing nice with him."

My parents always had my back when it came to something weird that I did, but they also always had advice for me.

My brother, Anoki, was a different story: he flat-out asked me why I liked Carlos. I didn't know that Anoki even knew him. He revealed to me that they played basketball in my school's park at times. He didn't agree with the degrading way that Carlos spoke about girls. Carlos didn't seem to have any respect for females.

Let me give you some background about this strange problem between Carlos and Anoki. Anoki was playing basketball with three of his friends at the park near our house when he saw Carlos walking by with a girl. They were arguing, and she got really loud and started screaming at Carlos about cheating. Anoki and his friends went over to them when they saw Carlos grab the girl by the arm and throw her to the ground. They had to pull Carlos off of the girl. He cursed them out and said, "Why don't y'all just mind your business." The girl was crying her eyes out, but Carlos seemed unaffected. Anoki told Carlos to leave her alone, and Anoki's friends knew her, so they walked her home. Meanwhile, Anoki said, Carlos got loud but then walked away.

This all happened about two months before I met Carlos. I couldn't imagine my sweet, wonderful guy hurting anyone.

My brother wasn't a liar, but I thought maybe there was a good explanation for it all.

One day when Carlos and I were talking at the pizza shop near our school, I asked him about the incident my brother told me about. Carlos told me that the girl was insisting he had gotten her pregnant, and he was mad because he couldn't possibly be the father. "There's no way I could be her baby's father," he said. "We only had sex once when we were dating. She's so stupid. Don't worry about her. She won't bother us."

Now, I know that a girl can have sex once and get pregnant. But at the time, I was so in love with Carlos that I went along with his story. I really wanted to believe him, and I didn't want to make a big deal about a girl who may or may not have been pregnant. Carlos said he was sorry the situation had me so upset. I just left it alone after that.

Later I decided to talk to some of my friends about the issue. Since it was Saturday, I went to Luisa's house, and Mercedes and Alicia met me there. We got together in Luisa's room to talk about what happened with Carlos. Mercedes, who was always the bold one, said, "Girl, he is so fine. You just need to keep tabs on him and keep asking the questions. I heard about him hitting his girlfriend in the park that day. You'd better stay close to him. You know guys are dogs."

I could tell Alicia was a little nervous about criticizing Carlos. "I know that you like him, but obviously something is wrong," she said. "I don't believe that the girl isn't pregnant. He may be lying, so you should investigate."

Luisa looked at me with deep concern. I think she hated to see me hurt, so she just decided to be honest with me. "When you first introduced me to Carlos, I knew there was something wrong," she said. "Anoki was right to tell you about him—he doesn't want you to get hurt. Carlos seems nice, but keep an eye on him. Remember this, if he could grab that girl in the park, who's to say he won't grab you? Be careful, and you know we've got your back."

My friends never let me down when it came to crazy guys, dumb girls, or even a bad hair day. High school was fun, but I probably wouldn't have enjoyed it as much without my friends.

CHAPTER 2

Can't Be Without My Carlos

By the end of the summer after freshman year, I had already gotten used to Chicago. I'd met so many people and made tons of new friends. That summer was great, and Carlos and I really got to know each other. We spent lots of time together going to amusement parks, seeing new movies, and going to the beach with friends. I loved summer in my new city, and I wished it could last forever.

But when the school year began, I knew it was going to be a good year. My classes were easy, I had great teachers, and my new homeroom teacher was really cool. The first day of school was major, because now I was a sophomore. I was psyched to show off my new clothes and light-brown highlights. Carlos liked the new denim miniskirt I wore for the first day of school. I couldn't believe that it actually passed my parents' inspection before I left the house.

Luisa, Mercedes, and Alicia were glad to see me, as I'd spent most of the summer with Carlos. Well, the beginning of sophomore year wasn't much different. Every day, Carlos walked me to school and back home. I didn't think it was a problem spending time with the man of my dreams, but all my friends seemed to think I was avoiding them. They would call me, and I wouldn't call them back for a week.

Orlana sat me down one day and said, "Carlos isn't worth losing all your friends. You never hang out with them anymore. When you lose all your friends, Carlos won't even care. He really isn't worth it." My sister is wise, and I have so much respect for her, but at the time I thought, *How could she possibly know how much I love Carlos?* My brother, Anoki, made me feel even worse. He came up to me later the same day and said, "You are an idiot if you can't see that Carlos is playing you. He has a baby, and he's an abuser. What is wrong with you? Open your eyes!"

And my parents were a lot more aggressive than either of my siblings. Mom said she couldn't figure out why I didn't see the warning signs when Anoki had to break up the fight between Carlos and his girlfriend. It turns out my mother had found out from Anoki that Carlos raised his voice a lot to me. This is what happened: It was right after school, and Anoki had just walked into the gym for basketball practice. Carlos and I were talking on the other side of the gym when I asked him about the rumors that he had a daughter named Tinequa. He blew up!. "Why do you believe these lies about me?" he yelled. "You always believe everything that people say about me!" Well, Anoki immediately ran over and screamed at Carlos so loud that I screamed back at Anoki. I looked at him, confused, and said, "Why don't you just leave us alone! Just stop it, Anoki!" Later I asked myself, *Why did you scream at Anoki that way when he was only trying to help you?*

My friends, who'd always understood me, now couldn't fathom why I was wasting my time with such a loser. Luisa, my closest friend, had stopped calling me or even speaking to me. It seemed like the more time I spent with Carlos, the farther apart Luisa and I became. One day I stopped her in the hallway at school and said, "What is your problem, Luisa? You never call me, I never see you anymore, and you've been so weird! What's going on?"

Luisa was very calm and direct with her words. "Morena, you are my best friend, and I love you. It makes me upset to see you with someone as horrible as Carlos. He is *el diablo*. I don't want to see you hurt, but you have to make up your own mind about this. Don't make it seem like we're to blame for this one. It was you who decided that Carlos was more important than your friends." Then she turned to leave without even waiting to hear what I had to say.

Could it be that I'd really messed up this time? I decided that Luisa was just being a bitch, and I let her walk away.

Mercedes and Alicia met with me after school that day. They were very candid about Carlos and held nothing back. Alicia really poured her heart out to me. She looked at me with her sad eyes and said, "Girl, I know you love him. It's just that I don't understand why you would date a guy that hits you and talks down to you. You are way too fabulous a person for him."

Okay, before I get to what Mercedes said to me, I need to back up and tell you what Alicia was talking about. Carlos and I were at Sherrelle's, a clothing store in the mall in my neighborhood, and Alicia happened to be passing by with her little sister when Carlos grabbed my arm and said, "You're stupid if you think that I'm paying for that ugly skirt." Actually, that wasn't the first time he'd done something like that. Carlos had become notorious for grabbing me and saying something to put me down.

Now that we were face to face, I could tell that Mercedes wasn't sure what to say to me. She had a concerned look, though. Finally she said, "You were always so sure of yourself. Anyone that would let dumb-ass Carlos put his hands on them needs to just kill themselves." Mercedes was a little extreme with her words, but she was right. I just wish that I had taken my friends' advice right after that conversation. Unfortunately, I stayed in my relationship with Carlos and tried to make it work.

One Thursday night, Alan, my best friend since childhood, called me. We hadn't seen each other since I left Portland, but I usually called him every Sunday. He was someone I could always talk to without feeling like I had to hide my true emotions. Alan knew about my relationship, since every time we talked, I went on about Carlos relentlessly. When he called me that Thursday night, though, I didn't mention my relationship because I didn't want Alan to judge me or think that I was stupid. I was a little shocked when we were chatting away and Alan suddenly said, "So … how is Carlos? Is he treating you right?" Just like that, he asked me those questions.

"He's okay. He's actually wonderful to me." At the time, I actually believed that. In my mind, Carlos was the greatest guy alive; however, to everyone else, he was the worst thing that could have ever happened to me.

"I always knew that you would find someone good for you," Alan said. "You are too cute to be with someone that doesn't treat you right."

I really felt confused after that phone call. To be honest, I think to this day that Alan wasn't convinced that everything was okay with me and Carlos. He knew me too well, and I could hear it in his voice.

Of course, having seen how my parents interacted, I knew a man wasn't supposed to treat a woman like crap. Mom and Dad might have had their disagreements, but they really loved each other. My dad had never laid a finger on my mom and never would. It's too bad I never noticed that before. I even watched how Orlana and her boyfriend behaved with one another. Lorenzo must have been Prince Charming, because he treated Orlana like a princess. He took my sister on a date every weekend, and sometimes he bought her nice gifts. That's what a good relationship should have been like.

Why was it so hard to be in love? All I knew was that I loved Carlos. Part of me knew that Carlos was wrong for treating me the way he did, but another part of me wanted to try and change him. I thought that if I just stayed with him, things would get better. When he grabbed me, it really hurt, but I figured he would change—he'd realize he was hurting me and just stop doing that to me. After all, he always apologized if I got mad at him for hurting me or for saying terrible things to me.

One Monday afternoon around five o'clock, when we were at the arcade by the school, he got mad at me for wanting to go home. I didn't think that it was a problem when I said to him, "Can we leave now, Carlos? I have a math test in the morning, and I want to study some more."

I was surprised when he blurted out, "Can't you see that I'm having fun? I never get to have fun. You're always complaining. Just stop acting like a spoiled brat!"

Really? All I kept thinking was that he was trying to impress his friends. He had totally spazzed on me just because I needed to get home. He grabbed my arm and took me outside, saying he needed to talk to me "in private." When we got outside, Carlos looked crazy. He was staring at the ground with his shoulders slumped forward. "What is the matter with you?" he said. "I didn't know that you would embarrass me in front of my friends like that. Denita, you are so spoiled. That is why I think I need to be tougher with you."

I didn't know what to think at that moment. What was I supposed to say? Maybe I should have stood up for myself. As I said before, I thought I could change him. How was I supposed to know that this dude was psycho? Our first two months together were heaven on earth. Then, after that, I began to notice how often he talked crazy to me. Oh, and did I mention that he slapped me once because he thought I was cheating on him? Yeah, I know. I was dumb for staying with him.

So why didn't I just go home without Carlos? That's a good question. The truth is that I really don't know. The school and the arcade are five blocks from my house. Maybe Carlos had a hold on me that I couldn't control.

That night, Carlos walked me home, but it was strange because he pretended that nothing had happened earlier. He played dumb the whole time.

Being the nice girlfriend that I was, I asked, "Are you okay?"

He said, "Of course, I'm okay. I'm walking with the most beautiful girl in the world. I'm sorry that I acted like such a jerk today. It will never happen again. I promise."

The interesting thing is that he'd said that before. He always apologized for mistreating me. He always treated me bad and then apologized for it. When he said he would never do it again, I'm guessing he meant he would hurt me every chance he got. Many times he would grab my arm so tight that I would fall to the floor because of the pain.

I felt so stupid. I never told my parents what was going on between Carlos and me, because they'd always taught me to have respect for myself. How would it look if I told them that Carlos had been doing those horrible things to me? What if they started treating me different? My sister, Orlana, was always encouraging me to do the right thing, Anoki couldn't understand what was going on in my head, my friends always told me the complete, honest truth, and I'd insisted to Alan that everything was fine. I was so confused; I didn't have any idea what was going on in my life.

Before Carlos became abusive, I felt invincible. Then, when the abuse started during our freshman year, I felt like disappearing into the world. I didn't know who I was anymore. When did I become the girl who lets her boyfriend smack her around whenever he feels like it? I felt so low that I didn't know how to lift myself up. I knew that my friends had my back if I needed help, but I felt so stupid that I didn't want to go to them for help, even when I felt hopeless. And by sophomore year, I did feel hopeless, because Carlos had really taken my self-esteem to a low point. I had no idea who I was anymore. I started doing things that didn't make any sense, like neglecting my friends to the point that they stopped speaking to me. My only school friend who would have anything to do with me was James.

James had a boyfriend, but we'd been friends since freshman year, and he always made time to spend with me. So one Saturday I confided in him about my crazy, mixed-up life. We met up at a Starbucks a few blocks from my house. I'd decided to tell him about how Carlos was treating me and how my friends didn't want anything to do with me. It was difficult to tell him about the big mess I was in, but I needed to do it. When James finally arrived at Starbucks, I felt as cold and clammy as though I were about to meet the president.

James sat down, looked at me, and said, "Denita, you are looking so scared. You look like you've just seen the Incredible Hulk. What's up with you?"

For a moment I stayed quiet. I knew I needed to be totally honest with James, since he'd been such a good friend to me.

"What's happening with you?" he said. "'I know that you haven't been hanging with Luisa anymore. You two were so close."

Finally muscling up the courage, I took a sip of my caramel macchiato and told James the ugly truth. "My life is a mess. It's a total wreck! My friends hate me, my family probably thinks that I'm stupid … I don't know what to do."

At first James looked into my eyes like I'd just told him that I was pregnant with quadruplets. I don't think he was surprised by my news, but he was probably confused that I'd decided to confide in him instead of Luisa. "I can't believe that your friends would hate you," he said. "Anoki told me that Carlos is bad news. You definitely shouldn't be with him if he's abusive. Of course, you know that I would find out if you didn't tell me." This is how the conversation went:

> ME: James, Carlos isn't who I thought he was.

> JAMES: Nita, what are you talking about? I thought you were in love with him. From what you told me before, he can do no wrong.

ME: I can't keep this up, but sometimes I
        don't know what I should do. I really
        believe that Carlos loves me. Maybe I
        just need to stop making him so angry.

JAMES: Wait one damn minute! Is Carlos
        hitting you?

ME, *not wanting to answer:* Since the
        beginning of sophomore year. I thought
        he would stop if I spent more time with
        him, but he just seemed to get worse.

JAMES: I can't believe this! What the hell are
        you doing with that asshole? Nita …
        Nita … I'm appalled. Why are you with
        this dude? He obviously doesn't care
        about you or he wouldn't be doing this
        to you.

That chat took hours. During our conversation, I
basically didn't know what to say to James but the truth.
I just spilled my guts to him, and I knew that he would
listen to me. I thought, *Maybe James can give me some
advice about everything.* Well, he told me to talk to my
parents and tell them what was going on. I couldn't do that.
I loved Carlos—he was fine! I know what you're thinking:
You idiot, listen to James! At the time, I was definitely

considering taking his advice and telling my parents, but I still didn't know what to do.

The next day, Sunday, I went with Carlos to see *Blood Bath Blues*. That's not what I wanted to see—I wanted to see *Under the Sun with Love*—but Carlos insisted. He hates romantic comedies. Anyway, after the movie I saw one of my friends from English class—Devante, James's best friend. Devante is tall, about six feet, and dark-skinned. He is gorgeous, but he was just a friend. Carlos was in the bathroom, and while I was waiting in the lobby for him, Devante and I were talking about the test we'd had the week before and how hard it was. When Carlos came out of the bathroom, he walked over to us, saying, "What's up, Devante? When are you going to join the football team? They need a good quarterback." Devante said that he'd be at practice on Tuesday, and then he got in his car and left.

Carlos and I walked to the diner down the street from the movie theater. Everything was fine until we'd finished eating. We were still sitting at the table when Carlos said, "Do you like Devante better than me now? I thought that you loved me. Do you think I'm blind or something?"

I was wondering when he was going to spazz on me about my friend. And that's all Devante was to me—just a friend. But Carlos had finally accused me of cheating on him again. I took a sip of water and was about to answer when he said, "So what's going on between you and Devante?" This is how that conversation went:

ME: Devante is one of my closest friends. You know he would never come between us.

CARLOS: Do you like him? Do you think he's cute? So … tell me what's up with you and Devante?

ME: Carlos, you know I love you. You always do this. Devante and I are *just friends*. I already told you this.

CARLOS: Why are you lying to me? (*Looking smug.*) I know you like him. I saw the way you looked at him.

ME: I was looking at him because I was talking to him. Calm down!

Okay, that conversation actually took a very long time too, but I finally convinced Carlos that Devante was just a friend. Just to give you an idea, this is how everything went:

1:00 p.m.: The movie, *Blood Bath Blues*, started.

3:50 p.m.: The movie ended.

3:57 p.m.: I saw Devante.

4:00 p.m.: Carlos and Devante began talking.

4:05 p.m.: Carlos and I walked to the diner.

4:46 p.m.: We were done eating.

4:50 p.m.: Carlos asked about Devante.

7:49 p.m.: I finally convinced Carlos that Devante and I were just friends.

8:14 p.m.: I arrived home.

I couldn't believe that it took me three hours to convince Carlos that I'd been faithful. Why did it take so long? I was so tired of trying to convince Carlos of something that he should've known already. He'd become so suspicious whenever I was talking to one of my guy friends that I had to sneak around just to talk to them. This wasn't normal behavior. I had to do something.

CHAPTER 3

Let's Talk About Things

A whole week went by before I decided that it was finally time to talk to my parents about my horrible life with Carlos. They seemed to think that he had some problems but was basically a nice guy, but he obviously had them fooled. He stayed on his best behavior whenever he came to our house. Everyone in the family would speak to him except Anoki; you couldn't pay my brother enough money to talk to Carlos. He knew the kind of guy Carlos was and didn't want any part of it. My parents always trusted me to do the right thing, so it was difficult to go to them about my problems when I didn't have any answers.

By now it was the spring of my sophomore year. The flowers were blooming and love was in the air. It wasn't in the air for me this time around. At this point, I thought my love life was drifting into nothingness. Everyone at school seemed so happy about spring. I wanted to feel that same joy, but I wasn't sure how.

One day I was taking all the clothes out of my gym locker so I could wash them, and James decided to approach me. He started off by saying, "So you didn't tell your parents about that fool?" Then, before I could answer, he said, "I knew it. You never even told them."

How could he have known how scared I was to tell my parents? I finally said, "How did you know that I didn't talk to my parents?"

He looked at me with a smile and said, "Because you would have told me by now."

James was right. I definitely would have told him if I had told my parents about Carlos. I tried to explain. "My parents expect so much from me. It would break their hearts if they knew how Carlos was treating me."

He looked at me with a concerned expression. "It would break their hearts even more if you kept this secret hidden from them. Tell your parents, Nita. They can definitely help you out of this jam."

Of course James was right, and I knew what I had to do. I geared myself up to talk to my parents that night. I didn't want to tell them anything; I wanted to handle Carlos on my own. But I also knew that I probably wouldn't be able to handle him, since he always got so angry at me. How had I allowed things to get this far in our relationship? I watched too much Lifetime television not to know that if your boyfriend is abusive, it's best to leave him. What was happening to me? Was I insane? Maybe I needed a psychiatrist or something. I just knew that I needed to tell my parents the naked truth.

After dinner, I told my parents that I really needed to talk to them about something. My mother looked worried, and my dad said with concern, "Sure, Nita. Let's go into the living room." We were just sitting down opposite each other on our plush sofas when Anoki and Orlana came in from the library. I asked them to please join us on the sofas. Anoki was a good big brother. He sat next to me on the sofa because he knew that the conversation was probably about Carlos, and he wanted to offer his support. No doubt feeling the same way, Orlana sat on my other side.

Dad started talking about how much he and Mom loved us, and how we could go to them about anything at all. I wasn't ready to talk yet, but I knew it was now or never. My parents were giving me their full and undivided attention.

I started talking about how much I loved them, and then I said, "Carlos and I ..." It took me a few seconds, but I finally decided to get everything off my chest. "I wanted to say that ... Carlos and I fight all the time. Everything seemed to be fine when we first met freshman year. It's just that ... it's just that ... well ... sometimes ... he ... he puts his hands on me."

My dad stood up, and my mother started crying. Dad blurted out with fire in his eyes, "Nita! What's going on? Is that bastard hitting you? Tell me, Nita!"

I had to say something, so I said, "Mom, please don't cry. Dad, this has been going on since the beginning of the year. I didn't mean for things to get this bad."

The mood in the house was astonishment and solidarity with a dash of anger. My parents said that they'd known something was going on with me, but when they'd asked me what was wrong I would say, "Nothing," and they didn't want to pressure me to talk more. I guess they figured that at some point I would come to them. Then Dad said, with a somber look on his face, "You are our daughter. We want you to be happy. You are not happy with Carlos, Nita." For some strange reason, I didn't respond. Maybe I should have said something so that it didn't look like I was defending Carlos.

Then Mom made a suggestion that probably would have solved my relationship problem: "Would you like us to invite Carlos over here and end things for you? Your father and I would be glad to do that."

Like a foolish girl, I said, "No. I think I can handle it."

My dad wasn't at all convinced of that. "Nita, are you sure? Because this is serious. You obviously don't know what Carlos is capable of doing."

I know now that my parents were right, but at the time I felt confident that I could handle the problem on my own.

Anoki thought I was stupid for not accepting our parents' help. After the family meeting, I went to my room to read a book, and he and Orlana knocked on my door about five minutes later. Anoki stood in my doorway and said, "Nita, that was dumb. You should've let Mom and Dad help you. Lord knows you'll never break up with that jerk."

Orlana was a little more pleasant but just as firm. She walked over and sat down on my bed. "Nita, if you don't break up with Carlos, you'll end up with tons of crazy problems. He's not worth it, *mija*."

I knew Mom and Dad were right. Anoki and Orlana stayed in my room for hours, until it was time for bed (around ten o'clock).

It had been a week since our family meeting. One Sunday afternoon, I got a phone call that took me completely by surprise. It was Luisa! All I kept thinking was, *OMG! It's Luisa!* Luisa hated that I was with Carlos. The whole gang wanted me to end things with him, but I wouldn't do it. The conversation between Luisa and me was interesting. Here is how it went:

LUISA: How are you?

ME: I'm good. I can't complain.

LUISA: When are you going to stop lying to yourself? You are in no way *good*. As long as you're with Carlos, your life will continue to go the way it's been.

ME: Luisa, stop it. Just because you don't like Carlos, there's no reason for you to treat me like this. Carlos is my boyfriend. If you don't like it, I don't know what to tell you.

LUISA: Girl, when are you going to wake up? Carlos is a straight loser. Why are you sticking around to be his bitch?

ME: *Bitch?*

LUISA: Yeah, you heard me. You're a serious tool. I love you, Morena, but damn it! Why are you staying with his dumb ass? He's so lame. Did you know about his baby?

ME: No, he doesn't have a baby. That's a lie!

LUISA: Excuse me, but yes he does. First of all, her name is Tinequa. I have seen her. The mother lives next door to me with her baby and parents. Yep, you'd better know it. Her parents were going to throw her out if she didn't stop seeing Carlos. He's bad news. The baby's mother is named Rhonda. She's really sweet, and Carlos cheated on her and treated her bad.

ME, *feeling cold inside.* Carlos is not cheating on me, so stop lying, Luisa!

LUISA: Oh really? So what about Brenda? Remember Brenda, the girl that can't stand us? She and Carlos are dating now. Brenda told me this while I was in the cafeteria one day last month. Carlos is bad news.

Luisa and I kept talking about how Carlos was no good, but I didn't want her to be right. I'd heard about his baby—even my parents knew about Tinequa—but I had no idea about Brenda. What could he possibly like about that girl? So what if she had a nice tan on her white skin, wore fake eyelashes, and had long, blond hair?

When I got off the phone with Luisa, I decided to go to Brenda's house since she lived right across the street. I didn't want to go, but my stomach just could not rest easy about the thought of her and Carlos together. Sure, Carlos was gorgeous, but that didn't give him the right to cheat on me.

As I was walking out the front door, my mom asked me where I was going. I had to tell her the truth. "I'm going to see Brenda across the street."

Mom gave me an confused look. "Baby, I thought you said that Brenda doesn't like you." She always knew what was going on at my school and with my social life. I told her that I was just going to ask Brenda something. She let me go, even though she probably knew why I was going.

I walked up to Brenda's door and was about to ring the bell when I heard Brenda call to me from her backyard, "Come back here, Denita!" This was definitely a weird turn of events. I never thought she would welcome me; she knew why I had come to her house.

Brenda was lying on a flowered lounge chair. I sat down on the matching one next to her. "So, you are here to discuss Carlos," she said. When I told her that I'd heard rumors about them going out, I wasn't ready for what she said next. "Carlos is an asshole! He approached me and said you and him are done. We went out for about a week, but then Mercedes and Alicia told me that you and Carlos were still together. Girl, when I heard that, I was furious. I cursed him out and I broke up with his lame ass. You don't have to worry about me even talking to that fool. Your friends really care about you. They told me how Carlos was treating you, and it turned my stomach. Sorry, Denita. You are way too nice for a dude like Carlos."

What? I was shocked to hear Brenda being so friendly. Usually she hated on me and whatever crew I was with, but she was nice when I was at her house. I even met her brother, Nicholas, and her parents. They surprised me too. Her mother was white and her father was Puerto Rican. It's funny, because she seemed *Boricua* to me.

Brenda and I hung out at her house the whole night. When I finally arrived home, I felt good, although I wasn't sure why. Maybe it was because I'd talked to Brenda about Carlos, or maybe I was glad that he wasn't dating her anymore. Yes, I'd made a new friend, but the issue with Carlos wasn't over. I wanted to confront him, I wanted to talk to him, but I was afraid to. Besides, he would just deny everything anyway.

The next day, when I was on the way back from my last class, I saw Devante. He was looking so good in his basketball uniform. The girls just loved Devante—not just because of his gorgeous face and chocolate skin, but because he was such a gentleman. He came from a very accomplished family. His mom was a doctor and his dad was an engineer. His brother was a sophomore at Bowling Green University, and Devante planned to go to college to be an architect.

Devante told me that he'd received a scholarship to play football at Shelvry University in Chickasaw, Texas. I was so happy for him. Then he told me that because of his accomplishments and good grades, his parents had bought him a BMW. A BMW—can you believe that? Devante was a year ahead of me, and I thought it must have been fantastic to drive a car as a junior in high school.

I think I'm talking too much about Devante. Actually, he and I were getting closer than ever, I guess because he was always walking over to me to talk.

About two weeks after my conversation with Brenda, Devante called me. I was lying on my bed, about to take a nap, when my iPhone rang. Devante was my secret crush, so when his name showed up on my phone, I started sweating like a pig in heat. Let me share how that eventful conversation went:

ME: I can't believe that you're calling me today. Wow! What a surprise!

Devante, *with swag in his voice.* Are you serious? We've been friends for a few years now. What's up?

Me: Not much. What about you?

Devante: You probably won't believe anything that I'm gonna say, but I was thinking about you.

Me: What? Don't you have a girlfriend? Don't make me have to knock you out, Devante. (*I was joking with him, as always.*)

Devante: There is definitely no girlfriend. Mercedes told me about Carlos. Are you alright?

We talked about Carlos, and I told him that it was hard breaking up with him. He couldn't resist saying, "Well, Carlos is all talk. I'm surprised that you're with such a loud-mouth dude like him." He went on to say that I was too good for Carlos, and then he said something that actually made me blush. "I've always thought that you were so beautiful. I know we're just friends, but I just wanted you to know that I have been attracted to you since you came to our high school."

OMG! I couldn't believe my ears. The awesome Devante was attracted to me? The guy was an all-star. What could he possibly want with me? Yes, he was handsome and cool, but I still had Carlos to deal with.

When it came to talking about guys, my mother was always the best person to talk to. After my call with Devante ended, I walked downstairs. She'd just finished sweeping the kitchen floor.

"Mom, I really need to talk to you," I said. I was smiling from ear to ear, so she was extremely happy to speak with me. I wondered if she could tell if it was about a guy, especially a guy other than Carlos. She told me to wait while she ran back into the kitchen to get us some ice cream. My mom was such a girly girl, and I loved her for that.

I told Mom that Devante was interested in me. She knew Devante because he was very good friends with Anoki. She said she thought highly of him and believed he was a true gentleman. Then she added, "Never peel a banana when one is already halfway open on the table." I was glad when she explained what the hell she meant by that Puerto Rican proverb. "If Devante likes you as much as he said he does, he will wait for you to break up with Carlos. Don't ever start a new relationship until you settle things with the older relationship. Carlos is bad for you, but your father and I want you to handle yourself with dignity. Devante is very sweet, but if he respects you, he'll wait for you."

My mom always had good advice about guys. After our talk, I decided that maybe I needed to start reaching out to more of my friends. I was determined to get them talking to me, no matter what it took to do that.

Why Does Luisa Hate Me?

My sophomore year had come to an end, and the summer air gave me such a sense of freedom that I felt like I needed to make some changes. Summer has always made me feel brand-new for some reason. I've never understood that, because most people feel this way in the spring. Well, I guess I'm just different.

When biology finally ended—it was my last class of the semester—Brenda caught up with me in front of school and invited me to a barbeque at her house at seven o'clock that Friday. I agreed to attend, and then she happened to mention that she'd also invited Alicia, Mercedes, and Luisa. She thought that it would be fun to invite the whole sophomore class to the barbeque. *Damn!* I really didn't feel like dealing with my friends right then, but I decided to go anyway.

About an hour before the barbeque, I decided to call Mercedes. I didn't feel like walking into an ambush with the crew. The conversation turned out to be a good idea, because Mercedes really treated me like a friend. She wasted no time jumping into things:

> MERCEDES: Girl, where in the world have you been? Did you talk to Devante? Girl, you need to get with him. Did you

see his BMW? That really needs to be your man.

ME, *giggling*. Mercedes, you are so crazy. How do you know that I need to be with Devante? Even if I did like him, it wouldn't be just because of his car!

MERCEDES: Okay, okay. Well, he told me that he likes you. Anyway, are you going to Brenda's barbeque? You know I definitely gotta get my eating on.

ME: Yeah, I'm going. Is Luisa going?

MERCEDES: You know she is, girl. I hope you talk to her when you see her. You know she's our girl.

ME: Luisa doesn't want to talk to me, and I don't even know if I have anything to say to her.

Mercedes was right. Despite my stubbornness, I knew that Luisa and I needed to talk, but I really didn't feel like hearing her tell me about myself again. When I got to the barbeque at seven o'clock, guess who I saw talking to Mercedes? You guessed it—Luisa! I wanted to go over there, but I decided to talk to James and his boyfriend instead. Did

I mention that James's boyfriend was a model? A cool diva! After a while, when I'd just finished playing volleyball with some friends in Brenda's backyard, Devante walked over to me and said with his cute smile (he had the whitest teeth I had ever seen), "Good form, Denita! Where'd you learn to play like that?" I told him that I always played volleyball in the summer. We decided to sit on Brenda's front porch, just to get away from all the loud noise for a minute. We ended up talking about everything, as usual. Then we had the conversation of the century:

DEVANTE: What's up with you and Carlos?

ME: I'm actually working on breaking up with him. He's not good for me anyway. It's because of him that Luisa won't even speak to me.

DEVANTE: You can break up with him. When Mercedes told me what was going on with you and Carlos, I have to say that I was surprised. You're so strong. You don't need a guy like him.

ME: Really? So what kind of guy do you think I should be with, Mr. Devante? (*I glance over at him flirtatiously.*)

DEVANTE, *grabbing both my hands and looking into my* eyes. You need someone that will be there for you … someone that won't hurt you or call you names. Basically, you need me. I know we've been friends for a while, but … Denita … you are so special. I hate that you're with Carlos. He's a terrible person! You can't possibly be happy with that punk bitch. I'm sorry, Denita.

ME: Awww, Devante. It's okay. I just don't know how to break up with Carlos. Come on, you know—one minute he's the sweetest guy; the next minute he's the devil. I don't want him to get angry at me. He just gets so angry.

DEVANTE: Maybe your friends should be there when you break up with him.

What Devante recommended made a lot of sense. I thought it was a good idea to have my friends with me when I broke up with Carlos.

When Devante and I finished our discussion, Devante had to go to his part-time job at Wendy's, so I went to Brenda's living room to watch *The Silent Deadly Man* with the rest of the group. We were halfway into the movie when I got a craving for another hotdog. I went into the kitchen and found Luisa there, pouring herself some cherry Kool-Aid. I picked up my hotdog, took a bite, and sat down at the table to eat while Luisa drank her Kool-Aid. When I was done eating and was getting up to go back in the living room, Luisa put her drink down.

Luisa: Wait, Morena. We need to talk. (*We sit down at the kitchen table.*) I just want to say that I'm sorry for treating you the way that I have. You don't deserve to be treated like a stranger.

Me: Okay, let's talk.

Luisa: I hate not talking to you. You have to understand, girl. Carlos is the reason why I haven't been around you. He's mean and crazy. You're always with him, and he knows that none of us likes him.

Me: Luisa, you have a right to your opinion. I actually think that it's time to break up with Carlos. (*I sound so sure of myself.*)

Luisa: Mija, what are you waiting for?

Me: I don't know. Maybe I need to do it soon.

LUISA, *sounding enthusiastic.* Hmmm …
Does Devante have anything to do
with this sudden change? (*She smiles
brightly.*)

ME: I'm guessing that Mercedes spilled the
beans on that one. I like Devante, okay?
He's sweet, smart, funny, and damn
fine. What's not to like about him? Girl,
I know that I need to break up with
Carlos. You know how he is. I don't
want him to do something crazy to me.

LUISA: Well, I'm here for you if you need
me. I love you like a sister.

After our conversation, Luisa and I hugged and went
back to the living room.

I was glad that I'd come to Brenda's barbeque, because
I got to see my friends. Luisa and I really needed to talk.
Carlos had drawn a wedge between us, and I couldn't let him
continue to do that. It was clear what I needed to do: I needed
to get away from Carlos. But how was I going to do that?
Could I just explain to him that we were not getting along?
I couldn't think of anything to say to him, because I knew
that no matter what I said, he would be angry. Everyone,
including my parents, was right about Carlos. It was time
to let it all go.

CHAPTER 5

Cut 'Em Loose ... Or Not

My junior year in high school had finally arrived. On a cool Sunday morning, I decided to call my best friend, Alan. He sounded so glad to hear from me. I told him about my summer in Puerto Rico with my family. Of course, I told him that I communicated with my crew by phone. Yes. I also told Alan that I called Carlos and treated him as though everything was fine between us. Alan was not happy about the Carlos situation, but he told me that he and his family had just gotten back from Barbados, where they are from. He'd sent me a Bajan flag as a souvenir. He is so good to me.

When I told him that I was trying to figure out how to break up with Carlos, he was very candid with his reply. "Why don't you just tell him to move the hell on? Nobody needs his ass anyway." After I finished laughing myself silly, I realized he was right. Why did I owe a long explanation to an unreasonable, abusive boyfriend?

Alan didn't get my fascination with Carlos. He reminded me about the time when I was twelve years old and a boy in our class pulled up my skirt, and I "dropped him like a bad habit" with my right fist. The boy never messed with me again. Alan couldn't understand how, if I could defend myself then, I could allow Carlos to take advantage of me now. I didn't know the answer to that one.

The next day, Monday, Mercedes stopped me in the hall as I was leaving art, my last class of the day, saying she needed to tell me about Carlos's baby issues. Alicia and Luisa met us outside so we could go to the nearby pizza shop together. As we were walking there, Mercedes couldn't resist telling us the details. "Carlos is in a serious mess. His baby's mother, Rhonda, told him that she has to move back to the Dominican Republic. So guess what? Carlos has to raise their daughter, Tinequa. The baby has to live with him and his parents. That's some deep shit that he's in."

The truth was that I had been avoiding Carlos. I knew that was wrong, but I still wasn't sure how to confront him. So I had no idea he'd been having issues like this.

Luisa, who really hated Carlos and couldn't have cared less about his baby, said, "Oh brother! He brought that on himself. Rhonda is a straight idiot for dealing with Carlos. They should have used protection or just not have had sex at all. They are totally screwed because Rhonda is going to the D. R. to stay."

Wow! I couldn't believe what I was hearing. *Carlos doesn't know anything about raising a baby* is what I was thinking the whole time. Maybe this was the perfect time to plan how to break up with him. I wasn't ready to be anyone's baby's mama.

Alicia agreed with Luisa but was a little more sympathetic. "Carlos and Rhonda have been together since the seventh grade," she said. "I like Rhonda, but I never could understand her and Carlos as a couple. I just feel sorry for that cute baby. Carlos may be a loser, but fatherhood could change him." Of course, Luisa and Mercedes didn't see any redeeming qualities in Carlos.

I had to admit it: I still loved Carlos. As misguided as my feelings were for him, part of me didn't want to lose him. So later, after I spent time with the girls, I did something very interesting. You won't believe it, but I'm going to tell you anyway: I called the infamous Carlos and told him that I loved him. Why did I do that? (I'm pretty sure that is what you're asking.) Well, the answer is that I have no idea. I guess I wanted him to know that I was here for him … and the baby. Yeah, I know. I was an idiot for calling him. Not to mention the fact that I was stupid to help him with the baby.

Of course, I soon regretted saying these things to Carlos. Within a few days, I found myself babysitting for him. We even took his daughter, Tinequa, to the park.

One day when I got home from school, Orlana asked me to come to her room so we could talk. "Why in the world are you still seeing Carlos, and why are you dealing with his baby?" she demanded. "You're acting crazy these days. Of course, you should know that this can get worse. Anoki was going to tell Mom and Dad, but I told him not to do that so I could talk to you. Come on, Nita!" As I sat on her bed, she went on to say that Carlos was obviously using me.

I knew that Carlos needed help with the baby, because he'd told me his parents had decided not to help him. They all lived together, but his parents couldn't believe that he would agree to raise Tinequa. Maybe in a way I just felt sorry for him.

Orlana was right though. I should've just let Carlos deal with his own situation. The only problem was that I was still his girlfriend; he expected me to be there for him. And none of my friends even liked him. Why was it so hard to let this guy go?

Well, every day it got harder and harder when I would spend time with Carlos. My weekends were spent entirely with Carlos and his daughter, Tinequa. I know what you're thinking—that I didn't learn anything from that disaster with my friends. And maybe you're right. Maybe I just needed to be bold and break it off with Carlos so that I could move on with my life. Time was definitely not on my side.

I knew that if wanted to learn to be bold, I had to get help, and the best person to help me was Mercedes. Mercedes was the most honest person I knew. She never had a problem sharing her feelings with someone. One time when we were in a store buying soda and she didn't like the price, Mercedes walked up to the cashier and said, "Excuse me, but this soda is too damn high. How do y'all expect to keep this store open with these outrageous prices? I may never come back in here again!" Do you know what happened? The manager came out and let her have the soda for free. Yes, that's right—free! Guess what happened next? The following week, the manager lowered the prices of certain items in the store, including the soda. You see what I mean? Mercedes was the "queen of the truth." I needed her help *now*!

I decided to invite Mercedes and the gang over that Saturday afternoon, since I needed help cutting Carlos loose. They all came upstairs to my room, and Mom brought us some snacks, since they'd be staying awhile. This will give you some idea of how it went:

> MERCEDES: I am so glad that you called me, girl. I was ready to break up with Carlos for you!

> LUISA: I hope you're serious this time, Morena. Carlos is too much of a dog.

> ME: I know. I'm glad you all came to help me. This is getting way out of hand. Carlos and I need to be done. He's driving me crazy.

> ALICIA: What about Devante? He should definitely be your man. He's such a gentleman. I can just imagine the two of you walking into the sunset together. (*She says this looking dreamy-eyed, her hands on her cheeks.*)

> ME: That sounds so nice to me, Alicia.

> MERCEDES: The first thing you should do is go over to Carlos's house and just

say, "We need to end this … *now!*"
He doesn't need a long, drawn-out
explanation. He's not worth your time.
We all know that.

LUISA: Don't tell her that, Mercedes. Look,
Morena, I know Carlos is a waste
of time, but you should still handle
yourself like the lady that you are. Talk
to him in a civilized way. (*Grinning at
Mercedes.*) I can't believe you told her
that.

ME: Okay, I'm confused now. I guess I
should take Mercedes's advice for a
clean break. I need out of this fast.

Our conversation went on for hours, and I still didn't
know what to do. That night, after my friends went home,
I called Devante. I know what you're thinking: I was being
crazy and underhanded for calling Devante instead of
dealing with Carlos. Well, that's not exactly what happened.
I called Devante because I wanted his opinion about how to
break up with Carlos. I figured that since he was a guy, he
would know how to handle the situation.

The next morning, Devante drove by to pick me up so
we could go to breakfast at IHOP. When I saw him, my
body went limp; I could barely stand up. Devante always
looked great because he had a fabulous sense of style, and

this morning he was wearing a gray Giorgio Armani sweat suit with brand-new white uptowns. Goodness gracious, he drove me absolutely crazy! He smelled like a dream too, since he was wearing Armani Code. That dude was a total stunner with the attitude of a poet.

We arrived at IHOP around nine thirty. I ordered my favorite thing, steak and eggs. He had chocolate chip pancakes. We were happy to see each another.

"Devante," I said, "you look and smell so good."

"I had to look good for you. I couldn't just wear anything." What an amazing response! I just melted in my chair. He took my hand. "You look really good yourself. You always look so amazing to me."

My heart must have been beating like a thousand times a minute. He was such the sweet talker. I kept thinking, *Oh, I love this guy.*

When Devante and I were done eating, we drove to a nearby park and sat by the lake. He was so romantic. I wished he were my man. He looked like he really wanted to speak to me. Finally he looked into my eyes and said, "What's going on with the Carlos situation? Are you still with him?"

I really wanted to say no, but I could never lie to Devante—I cared too much about him. I just told him that I was having a hard time breaking up with Carlos. Why was it hard for me to break up with such a loser?

Devante was patient with me though. "Denita, you're a bright girl—you know what's best for you. Carlos is not what's best for you. I really want to be with you, but you have to cut him loose." Those words sounded so simple to my ears, but the fact remained that I was a straight-up coward for not breaking up with Carlos.

Devante and I stayed at the park, just talking, for about five hours. He was very vocal about Carlos being the wrong one for me and how he wanted me to do the right thing. So I knew what I needed to do, even though I was still afraid.

Then something happened that would change my life forever. It finally happened: *the kiss.* Yes, his lips landed on my lips as we were discussing the school mascot. I know that's a weird conversation to be having, but Devante must have thought that it was a perfect time to lay the big one on me. His lips were soft and smooth, and he held me so close to him that I felt like we were already a couple. I didn't want that moment to end. Devante made me feel like I was on a tropical island with a warm breeze blowing through my hair. That kiss was truly magic. Devante's lips were definitely lethal.

Devante and I drove back to my house, and he walked me to my porch. Before we said good night, Devante said, "You will always be my friend, no matter what you decide to do." As we were hugging, my mother "conveniently" opened the door very slowly and greeted Devante. How embarrassing! Devante was a gentleman with my mom, and they exchanged a few kind words. He said that he would call me, and then he drove off in his BMW.

It was obvious that Devante had left a lasting impression on Mom. "Devante is so nice," she said. "Remember what I told you. Come clean with Carlos first." My mother was so right. I decided that I'd break up with Carlos Monday at school. That way everyone would be around, and he wouldn't make a scene—or so I thought.

When Monday finally arrived, I ran into Mercedes in the hall after third-period English. She wanted me to tell her about my date with Devante. Of course I told her everything. Then she brought up the subject of Carlos. She knew I hadn't broken up with him, because I hadn't told the group. She scolded me (I couldn't believe it) and said, "Look, girl, Devante is the one for you. Carlos is a jackass. Wake up!" I just stood there like a deer in headlights. Then the bell rang and we went on to fourth period.

Mercedes is so right, I thought. *Why can't I just take her advice?*

When eighth period ended, I saw Carlos coming out of his class. He was walking toward me, but so was my crew— Mercedes, Alicia, and Luisa. What a dilemma! My friends wanted me to end things with Carlos, and Carlos had no idea what was going on.

Mercedes said to me, "You know we have your back, girl. Do yo' thang!" Luisa and Alicia looked at me with gentle smiles. I felt confused and sick to my stomach for some reason.

Carlos hugged me and said, "What's up?" to my friends. Then he said, "You coming with me or them?"

I wanted to go with him to keep the peace, but I just blurted out, "Wait!" That beginning sounded strong, right? Well, I sort of crashed and burned. This is what happened:

CARLOS: Wait for what?

ME: I think I should just go with my friends.

CARLOS: Come on, we can go to the pizza shop. We always go to the pizza shop after school. What's the problem?

MERCEDES, *without an ounce of fear in her voice.* If Nita doesn't wanna go with you, what's the problem with that?

LUISA: Morena, you know what to do. Don't you have something to tell Carlos?

CARLOS: Tell me what, Nita?

ME: Ummm … (*I feel like I'm in the Wild West and this is showdown time.*) I think that … it may be time to … well, I think …

MERCEDES: Oh brother! Look, I can't take you two any longer. Carlos, Nita wants to break up with you. You're abusive, and no one needs you. Least of all Nita.

> LUISA, *sounding angry.* That's right!
> She's our friend and we love her. You
> definitely don't love her like we do.

> CARLOS: Is that true, Nita? Nita?

Well, what could I say? My friends were right, but I felt so awkward. I knew that Carlos was bad for me, but somehow I still couldn't break up with him. I wished I had their boldness. To tell you the truth, I felt like a shy little girl, with my friends on one side of me and Carlos on the other. I stood in the hall that day like a dead fish. "That's true, Carlos," I said softly.

There. I finally did it. I just wished this didn't happen:

"Oh, so your friends are making the decisions about us now? Nita, tell me you're joking so we can get outta here."

I couldn't move a muscle.

"Oh, you don't want to go with me now? This is why I can't stand your friends!"

My friends were looking at Carlos with total disgust. I could tell they were ready to hurt him. This is what happened after Carlos uttered those terrible words:

> MERCEDES, *putting her right hand over her
> heart.* First of all, Nita is our friend. We
> have her back. Do you? I should kick
> your ass! We don't like you either, so
> the feeling is mutual.

CARLOS: Shut up, Mercedes! Nobody needs
    your mouth in this!

MERCEDES: Go away, Carlos, with your bitch
    ass! Take a hint and bounce!

LUISA, *really angry.* Carlos, you are nothing
    but trouble. Why can't you just leave
    Morena alone? Haven't you done
    enough? You're pathetic!

MERCEDES: That's right! You're such an
    asshole! (*She just loves to curse.*)

CARLOS, *turning to me with a sweet voice.*
    Make a decision, baby. Me or them?

What? I had no idea what to do. If I went with my
friends, Carlos would blame them. If I went with Carlos,
my friends would hate me. I needed to decide, and for some
stupid reason, I went with Carlos. I told my friends that
I would call them later. That's when Carlos and I left the
school with his arm around my shoulders. I felt like an
idiot—I guess because I *was* an idiot for going with him
instead of my friends. I was also an idiot for not breaking
up with him. Was this ever going to end?

CHAPTER 6

Help! My Life Is a Mess!

Two days had passed since that travesty of a Monday, when I thought I was breaking up with Carlos. I didn't go to school Wednesday because I had an appointment for a routine checkup, so I basically stayed in the house the rest of that day. Nothing could make me forget about that awful fiasco, the showdown between Carlos and my crew. My friends did call me though. They understood that I was trying to keep the peace by leaving with Carlos that day. To be totally honest, I really didn't want to leave with Carlos. Let's face it—I'm a serious coward who needs to be slapped. Mercedes had given me some good advice. Why didn't I take it?

On Thursday night, miraculously, James came over to see me around seven. He was very much loved by my family, and he and Anoki were always together, usually playing basketball and talking about girls (even though Anoki knew that James is gay). I sometimes sat in with them to see if I could maybe learn something from them, or criticize them about something that they'd said. All I knew tonight was that James and I obviously needed to talk, since he'd come all that way just to hang out with me.

James and I went to the living room to talk. He wasted no time opening his mouth to me. "So what's going on with you and Devante? He and I are best friends. You had to know that he was going to talk about you."

James and Devante had talked about me? Why? Well, we were all friends; I guess there wasn't any harm in them talking about me. "Okay, spill it," I said. "What has Devante been saying about me?" James just couldn't stop smiling. I nudged his arm as if to say, "You're so crazy."

Alan and James reminded me of each another. Alan always thought he knew what was best for me, and James always gave me advice about my life. Was my life so hard to manage that I needed three fathers? I knew James and Alan meant well, so I never got mad, and I usually took their advice. But I wish I had listened to them about Carlos. I often wonder whether, if I had told them what was really going on in my life, I might have avoided this Carlos situation. James absolutely hated Carlos. He never said a word to him. When James saw Carlos and me together, he would speak to me as though Carlos wasn't even there. Is that rude? Maybe. James had his reasons though. Like my childhood friend, Alan, he was very protective of me. He hated to see me unhappy or hurt.

Okay, so you're probably wondering, *If you were so unhappy, why were you still with Carlos?* That is a really good question. Was it fear that was keeping me with Carlos? What could he possibly have done to me? Carlos wasn't exactly the most powerful dude in the world, so what was my problem? Questions, questions, questions … and my life was a mess.

Around two o'clock that Thursday, while I was in biology, I got this text message from Mercedes: "Muchacha, I hope you know that Carlos is in the hallway right now with the police. I think that they might arrest him for whatever reason."

What? Carlos was no angel, but why would he be arrested? Was it because of me? As much as I should have been taking credit for calling the police, I really hadn't called them. After school, me and my crew met in the gym. Luisa didn't see everything, but she usually made it her business to find out what she needed to know about the school. This is the conversation that she couldn't wait to have with us:

> ME: Mercedes, please tell me that they didn't arrest Carlos.

> MERCEDES: Girl, I wish that I could say yes to that one. That fool is so lucky that I didn't call the cops on him.

> LUISA: That fool was snitched on someone about something. He's not exactly squeaky clean. He's had his share in the criminal game. Robbin', stealin', you name it! He's a waste of space!

> ME: I never wanted him to go to jail. I just want him to leave me alone.

ALICIA: We've already decided to help you
with that. You're our friend, and we
can't keep letting these things happen
to you.

MERCEDES: His ass is mine if he suspects
that I had anything to do with the police
talking to him.

LUISA: Anyway (*looking at Mercedes and
then at me*), when you are ready to do
this break-up with Carlos, we'll be right
there with you.

*I just stand there and cry. Then we do a nice
group hug.*

MERCEDES: That's right Nita. We won't leave
you! Never!

When I got home after school, I couldn't wait to tell
everyone that Carlos had been questioned by the police.
Rumors around school were that he was accused of assaulting
a girl, but nobody knew who.

After I talked about it to my family, I went upstairs to
get started on my homework. Anoki stuck his head in my
bedroom door. "So … were you wondering who told on your
boy Carlos?" He had a smirk on his face. "It was anonymous,
of course."

I couldn't help but look at him and say, "*No!* Oh wow, Anoki. Well at least you didn't say it was me. I guess I should thank you for that much."

"I was going to tell them it was you, Nita, but I didn't want to get you involved. He'll get what's coming to him one way or another. See ya." He left to go downstairs to the kitchen.

Wow! I always knew that my brother cared about me, but I never knew that he would call the police on Carlos.

Well, that one incident caused mass hysteria. My phone rang all evening. Everyone except my crew was calling me about Carlos, asking questions like "What happened?" or "Did he kill someone?" or even "Is he in danger?" It was crazy! I couldn't believe the mess that was going on around me, all because of Carlos. What had I gotten myself into?

James called me around nine o'clock that night, after everyone had stopped calling me and I was finally done with my homework. He said, "Girl, what in the world is going on with Carlos? The police were going in on him. I saw it with my own eyes. Did he hurt you again?"

I told him how Anoki had called the police as an anonymous tipster about an assault on a girl in our high school. James was so protective of me. He was like a brother to me, so I wasn't too mad that he was asking me questions about Carlos and that weird fiasco. I assured him that things were good, but he could see right through that. I didn't know what to do anymore. I was just glad that I had my friends around me. This breakup had to happen!

The next day, Friday, my crew decided to pick me up so we could all go to school together. As we walked to school, Luisa told me, "We came to get you this morning because we didn't want you going anywhere with Carlos. Have you spoken to him since yesterday?"

I told her that I was avoiding him. He must have called me like thirty times the night before, and around three thirty in the morning, he texted me, saying, "Baby, I didn't do anything. Please call me."

They weren't surprised. Mercedes looked at me with her hazel eyes and said, "He contacted you because you are the only one who likes him besides his daughter and his family and friends. Nobody has time for his ass."

Luisa immediately said, "Actually, I'd love to know who called the police on him. He is such a loser."

Alicia put her arm around me and said in her sweet, angelic voice, "Does Devante know what's going on?" I couldn't help but smile and giggle at that comment.

I glanced at Luisa and whispered, "Anoki made an anonymous call to the police." Then I said to Alicia, "I will call Devante tonight."

When I was in third-period Spanish, Luisa texted me: "Girl, I haven't seen Carlos. Is he in school today?"

I knew she'd asked about him because she wanted me to break the news to him that day. She usually saw him in front of the lockers around third period; he hung out with the same guys every day at that time. It didn't matter to me, but it was weird to Luisa. I texted her that I would come to her next class to talk.

When I got there, she and I walked up to Carlos's friend Pedro and I said, "Hey, have you talked to Carlos? He's usually here with you guys."

At first he just gave me a shocked stare. Then he finally said, "What's up, lovely ladies. Carlos said he needed to leave town for a while. I think it had something to do with the police questioning him this week. He didn't say where he was going though. His mom has the kid."

So Carlos skipped town, I thought. *That's interesting.* Where could he have gone? The Dominican Republic? Puerto Rico? New York City? Miami Beach? Where was this dude? He usually called me. Was he ever going to call me again? Why did I even care?

This could be a good thing. If there was no Carlos to be found, there would be no reason to break up with him. On the other hand, I doubted he would not complete the school year. During eighth-period math, I couldn't even concentrate; I just kept thinking about where Carlos could be. It was only one day, but he would usually call if he wasn't going to be in school. Shouldn't I have been happy that he was nowhere around? Maybe. My feelings were definitely mixed. This seemed like such a complicated issue.

Around six o'clock the Friday of the following week, I had just walked in the door from school and was sitting down for dinner with my family when there was a knock at the door. Dad got up to answer it. The rest of us were laughing and talking when he came back into the kitchen and said, "Nita, the police are here to speak to you."

Oh no! I thought. *This is probably about Carlos.* What was I going to say to them? Well, Dad agreed to sit with me while I talked to them. Mom, Anoki, and Orlana stayed in the kitchen to eat their dinner, because Dad assured them that he would handle it.

My father and I put our plates in the warm oven and went into the living room to speak to the officers. We all took our seats on the couches that faced each other—the two officers sat across from Dad and me. One officer said, "Hello, Denita. I am Officer DeWitt, and this is my partner, Officer Ramirez. We have to ask you some questions about your boyfriend, Carlos."

Why was this happening? Why couldn't Carlos just be a nice guy?

"What exactly is this all about?" my dad blurted out.

"We decided to follow up on the anonymous call about Carlos Lugo abusing a student in the local high school," Officer Dewitt said. He looked at me. "Teachers are saying that you two are dating. Is that true?"

I really wanted to say no. I took a few seconds to tell them yes.

"Nothing will happen to you if you are dating him," Officer Ramirez interjected. "We just have to monitor this situation, because we have seen too many abusive teen relationships end badly. We're talking death here."

Mom came in to join us, while Anoki and Orlana went off to their rooms. She sat next to Dad and held his right hand as she greeted the two officers. Then she kept quiet and let him take control. Dad looked at me and said, "Nita, if you have something to say to these officers, the time is now."

I felt a little weird. Officer DeWitt was a man, so I figured he wouldn't understand. But Officer Ramirez was a woman, so I thought maybe it was time to talk.

CHAPTER 7

Carlos Is Back. Now What?

Junior year was full of surprises. When Carlos came back to school, it was September. It had been two months without Carlos, and everything seemed easy without him around. I figured that since I couldn't get in contact with him, there was no cause for alarm. I was glad that I didn't have to break up with him. But one morning around nine o'clock, when I was at my locker, Carlos walked up to me, grabbed my face, and kissed me right dead in the mouth. He seemed so happy to see me.

"Hello, sweetheart," he said gently. "I know that I should have called you. I had to get out of town for a while. I went to Atlanta to visit my brother Alonzo. I did miss you though."

Maybe you need to hear the rest of that crazy conversation. Here it is:

> ME: If you missed me, you would have called. You didn't even say you were leaving. What am I supposed to do with that?

> CARLOS: Baby, the police were all in my business. I wasn't trying to hide, but I needed to clear my head. I knew

you would have a hard time with me leaving, so I left in a hurry. I didn't like doing that to you. (*He grabs my waist with his left hand and caresses my cheek with his right hand.*)

ME: I wasn't sure you broke up with me or not. I did call you though. (*I shouldn't have, but I did—sue me.*) You put me through so much these last two months.

CARLOS: I know, Nita. I'll make it up to you. We can talk tonight—I'll call you later.

ME: Carlos, why can't we just talk after school?

CARLOS: Hmmm, I have some things I have to do. I'll call you tonight. (*He kisses me and gives me a hug.*)

At this point, Carlos was at the end of the hallway, and Mercedes was passing by me on her way to class. "That fool just came in the building and came straight to you," she said. "Maybe you need to break up with him sooner rather than later."

I told her that it would get done. Carlos had just gotten back, so time was on my side—or that's what I thought, anyway.

When I was talking to Carlos, he'd seemed different. Had his trip changed him? He seemed a lot more patient in his tone—maybe because I had been without him for two months, and I was blinded by his kind gestures. That surely may have been the case. I wanted to know whether Carlos was up to something or was just being nice for now. I really had no idea what to expect.

After school, Carlos and I walked to the local pizza shop. I needed to know so many things about what was going on with him. When we finally sat down in a booth with our pizza slices and sodas, Carlos wiped his mouth with a napkin and said, "Nita, the police are still bothering me. They called my mother yesterday about me. She screamed at me, saying 'Who is this girl that you are hitting? You'd better not be in any mess. I run a good home here.' It was a disaster yesterday." I wasn't shocked at that news. Then he said, "Nita, did you call the police on me? You know that I love you. I don't mean those things that I do. You're my sweetheart."

I told him that it wasn't me who'd called the police. I didn't mention that the police had come to my house to talk to me about him. I really didn't need him angry with me at that moment. I just sat with him to have a nice chat, and after we were done talking, he walked me home.

My crew met me at my house so we could do our homework together. Of course my mother had already fixed them some sandwiches and juice—she liked my crew. They were eating in my room when I walked in.

Alicia said something so crazy: "Nita, your brother is so cute. How old is he?" Mercedes and Luisa were waiting for me to answer that interesting question. First I laughed out loud, and then I fell over backward, since we were on the floor anyway. I told them that he was nineteen and a freshman at Hullman College on the Northside. My crew thought my brother was a god.

At that point Anoki came to my bedroom door and said in suave voice, "Hey, girls. What's going on?"

Oh brother, I thought. My crew swooned as he stood in the doorway. They all smiled at him, and Mercedes gave him a hug. Goodness gracious. My brother was good-looking, charming, sincere, and athletic—and probably more things—but give me a break.

Anyway, while I was doing my homework with the crew, I received a nice text message from Devante: "How are you, beautiful? I thought about you all day." Wow, what a text! We had been talking on the phone ever since Carlos left.

I immediately texted him back. "I'm doing good. I'm just doing homework with the crew. I've been thinking a lot about you too."

Mercedes looked up at me with a curious grin. "What's happening right now?" she asked. "Why are you smiling? Is that the gorgeous Devante?"

Luisa flashed her cute smirk and said, "What did our boy say?"

After I read them his text, they couldn't resist talking about him.

Alicia, who really wanted Devante for me, said, "Girl, when are you going to swoop him up? He's liked you since freshman year. We're about to be seniors. What's the deal?"

Mercedes had to have a piece of the action too. "Nita, he is fine! If he liked me, I wouldn't waste any time like you are. Por favor, chica. What are you waiting for?"

Good question, right? Yeah, I thought so. "I don't know," I said.

Luisa had on her serious face—no smile. "I know. It's that damn Carlos. Morena, the girls are right. What's happening? Do you still love Carlos or something?"

Did I still love Carlos after all that we had been through? When I didn't answer Luisa, the crew stopped smiling and just looked at me. What could I say? I did still love Carlos.

After about eight seconds of silence, Alicia said, "Let's just finish our homework," and that's what we did. I felt like an idiot.

That morning I'd gotten excused from Spanish class to go see my guidance counselor, Mrs. Gandolfini. I asked to see her because it was getting harder and harder to break up with Carlos. When I entered her office, she asked me to have a seat in the chair on the other side of her desk. This was our chat:

MRS. GANDOLFINI: How are you, Denita?

ME: Hello, Mrs. Gandolfini. I'm good. It's just that … well … I don't know what to do.

Mrs. Gandolfini: I'm assuming you're referring to Carlos.

Me: Yes, ma'am.

Mrs. Gandolfini: Denita, based on what you told me last week, Carlos isn't the problem. The problem lies within you. You may have problems knowing what love is. Love is not abuse. Love is kind. It helps to have an example. (*She begins writing in her notebook.*) How's the relationship between your parents?

Me: They really love each other. My father asked my mother to marry him when he was twenty and she was eighteen. He said that he just "knew." I don't really understand that.

Mrs. Gandolfini: You don't have to understand that yet. It sounds like you have a great example of love right there in your own home. Your parents sound a lot like my husband and me. We were twenty-three when we got married. Now we're in our fifties, with four children. What did you expect to gain from your relationship with Carlos?

ME: I guess I wanted him to be like my father, or at least like my brother, Anoki. In the beginning of our relationship, Carlos was sweet, but now there are times when I don't understand him. It's just that he gets so angry at me. Sometimes I don't even know what I did. I know that I need to break up with him. I just don't know how.

MRS. GANDOLFINI: What about your friends—or your crew, as you referred to them? You told me that they would be there for you when you broke up with Carlos. I think that is a great idea. You obviously can't do it without the support of your friends. Utilize them. They definitely care about you. Trust me on that.

ME: I wish it was that easy. (*It really is, actually.*) But you're right, Mrs. Gandolfini.

Our conversation lasted for about an hour. I really admired Mrs. Gandolfini—not because her husband was a rich Italian stockbroker in Chicago (he'd come to our career day that month, and Mrs. Gandolfini had introduced him to me and my crew), but because she was very well-groomed and polished. She looked a lot like Viola Davis. She had her master's degree, and it just seemed nice that I was getting advice from such a great woman. Mrs. Gandolfini was a very smart lady, and she'd told me that I had the brains to go to any college I wanted. I'd told her that me and my crew were definitely going to college. She was very pleased and offered to help me any way she could. Mrs. Gandolfini was the best guidance counselor ever.

When I arrived home, the house was quiet. I had just left my crew, and it was only Anoki, Orlana, and me in the house. Orlana said that Dad had taken Mom out for dinner and a movie. That's when I decided I'd had enough: I wanted what my parents had. Carlos needed to be history. It was time to end things.

CHAPTER 8

Who's It Going To Be—
Carlos or Devante?

As I told you before, Devante and I had been texting and calling each other for weeks, ever since Carlos left town. It was so exciting getting to know him. Although I did feel a little guilty, Devante never made me feel that way. He said that I didn't have anything to worry about because he had nothing but respect for me. Besides, Carlos needed to be history anyway.

One Thursday when I was walking to the cafeteria to meet the crew, Devante stopped me in the hallway. I was so happy to see him there with his handsomeness just surrounding me. This fine dude standing in front of me made me feel so safe. Well, I asked him what was going on, and he said, "Hey, Nita. What are you up to this Saturday? I was hoping that we could get together."

It's not like I hadn't been out with him before, so of course this date wouldn't have been any different. It's just that I really needed to sort things out with Carlos first. I felt like a cheater running around with two guys. That wasn't right. So I didn't even hesitate when I looked into Devante's big, brown eyes and said, "Devante, as much as I really like you"—even though I loved him—"I think that it would best for me not to go out with you."

Devante gently grabbed my hands and stared into my eyes. "Aww, why, beautiful?"

Wow! I felt like I could have just melted onto the floor after that comment. I let him hold my hands while I stared into his eyes and said, "Because if I want things to feel right between us, I really need to break up with Carlos. Trust me. I know what I'm doing."

Devante was a gentleman, and he handled my conversation with sincerity. This is how our charming discussion went:

> DEVANTE: Okay, how are you dealing with that? I knew he was still in the picture.

> ME: Devante, you should definitely be my man. I know that, but things are weird because of Carlos. I promise to break up with him soon.

> DEVANTE: Nita, you are brilliant, so I'm sure you know what you're doing. I love you—I can wait. I just want the best for you, but I don't want to rush you either. If you need my help with Carlos, just give me a call.

Wow! What a wonderful guy. Well, I definitely felt like a princess. Devante kissed me on my forehead and jetted away to his BMW. I couldn't help running to my crew in the cafeteria. I ran toward them, sat down on the floor with them, and screamed out, "I love Devante!" They all smiled at me like I'd won the lottery.

Mercedes stopped sipping her soda and said, "Girl, Devante is your man. I been told you that."

Luisa said in her motherly voice, "First things first. Let's deal with one thing at a time. Remember Carlos?"

Man! I already knew that I needed to break up with Carlos. I really didn't need to hear that right then. Let me set the record straight: I wasn't mad at Luisa for saying that about Carlos. I was mad at myself for handling things wrong. But since speaking to Mrs. Gandolfini, I felt much more confident about the situation. Ending my relationship did seem easier to do. I just needed to do it.

When my crew dropped me off at home, my mother was waiting for me in the living room. I don't think I ever saw her look so concerned about anything until that moment, when she said to me, "Have a seat, sweetheart. Have you been having trouble with Carlos?"

I knew Mom was going to talk to me about this someday, so I had a seat on the couch across from her and reassured her. "Mom, I knew I needed help, so I talked to Mrs. Gandolfini. She said that using my friends to help me was the best idea, so that's what I'm going to do. Don't worry, Mom." My mother never really needed to worry about me most of the time, but this Carlos situation really had her scared. I couldn't blame her.

I stayed in the living room to do my homework while my mom watched some crazy novela on television that she liked. Around seven, Orlana came in from college with her boyfriend. He greeted me and Mom, and then he and Orlana went into the kitchen. As I did my homework, I could hear them laughing while they ate dinner together. They sounded so happy. My dad came home around eight; he'd been doing some overtime at work. He said hello to us, passionately kissed my mom, and said to her, "I missed you all day." Then he kissed her again. There was so much love around me. Isn't that what I wanted—a nice relationship with someone who cared about me? Didn't I deserve that? Why was I so blind? Carlos didn't love me, and it was time I did something about it.

By now October had crept up on us. It was Sunday, and I was sitting in my room writing in my diary. I'd kept a diary since I was seven years old. Lately, I had been writing a lot about Carlos. I had also had been writing about Devante. It was weird, juggling two guys. Well, Devante had told me that we couldn't go on any more dates until I got Carlos out of my life. He wasn't pushing me, but I felt that I needed to do something fast. The pressure was on.

After I finished writing in my diary, I called Mercedes. Luckily for me, the rest of the crew was at her house, so I didn't have to tell the story multiple times. When I explained to Mercedes that I needed their help to break up with Carlos, she quickly replied, "Of course, girlfriend. We'll meet you at your house."

This was it. I was finally about to break up with Carlos. Did I know I was going to do it? Of course not. I guess I was relying on the strength of my crew for help. The moment I told Mercedes what I needed to do, I felt my heart sink into the floor. What was I about to do? I still loved Carlos—was this the right thing to do? I knew that I probably wouldn't be able to go through with it, so I started to call Mercedes back. But just as I picked up my phone, I heard the doorbell ring. I was hoping that it wasn't the crew, but it was.

Mercedes was excited that I had finally decided to go through with the breakup—my whole crew was happy for me—but that happiness was short-lived. "I can't do it!" I said.

They all stared at me, more confused than I'd ever seen them. Mercedes sat on the living room couch with her face in her hands. Luisa sat on the couch looking stunned. Alicia walked over to me and shouted, "Nita! What is going on? I thought that you were really going to do it this time!"

I wasn't sure how I felt at that moment. On the one hand, I knew that I needed to be done with Carlos. On the other, I wasn't sure of the outcome. Then it finally happened, the moment that I knew would change everything: James rang the doorbell.

Mercedes jumped up and opened my front door. James ran in excitedly and said, "Yeah, girl. It's Carlos's ass today!"

"How did you hear about that?" I asked.

"Mercedes called me right after you spoke to her," he said. "So are we going over to Carlos's house right now? Should we kick his ass?"

Mercedes saw that I couldn't really say anything. She looked at James. "Sorry, boo. Miss Nita decided not to go through with it. We could've kicked his ass together."

I already felt weird, but that didn't stop James from scolding me. "Oh my lord, Nita. What the ... okay. Why did you decide to back down now? You know you're not happy with Carlos." The discussion continued:

> JAMES: What is it about Carlos? I can't stand his ass.

> LUISA: None of us like him. Morena, why?

> ME: I wish I could explain.

> JAMES: Well you need to, girl. Carlos is abusive, stupid, lazy, and a punk bitch. He is no good for you. Why do you want that dumbass? (*HIs mouth is just as bad as Mercedes's.*)

> ME: I ...

LUISA: She's scared. Morena, why are you scared of Carlos? Just get Anoki to punch him in the face.

ALICIA: Maybe she's afraid that Carlos will hurt her. He won't, though. He knows that the cops are on him.

MERCEDES: That's right, Nita. Come on!

JAMES: Girl, I came all the way over here because I thought you finally got hold of some sense. It turns out that you don't have no idea what's going on.

MERCEDES: Yeah, Nita. What's going on? *Are* you scared?

ME: I just don't know if it's the right thing to do because …

MERCEDES: Because you probably still love Carlos.

JAMES: Damn! Look, Nita, what do you want? I guess it's okay to still love him, but you can't change Carlos. He has put you through enough.

ME: I know, but …

JAMES: There's no buts. Carlos needs to go. I
know you definitely want to end things
with him. It's now or never, Nita.

ALICIA: James is right, Nita. We all love you
and hate to see you hurting because of
something Carlos did to you.

LUISA: Yes, we love you, Nita. Let us help
you bring this bastard down.

ALICIA: Luisa …

LUISA: Sorry. Let's bring Carlos down. (*She
and Alicia smile at each other.*)

MERCEDES: That's it, Luisa! You got it, girl!
(*Putting her fist in the air.*) Bring that
bastard down!

JAMES, *in his calm, gentle, raspy voice.*
We're with you, Nita. Please don't be
afraid.

As I sat on the couch, thinking about what everyone
had said, Anoki and Orlana walked past us. They were on
their way out of the house to catch the movie matinee down
the street. "Hey, guys," Anoki called. "Nita, you coming?"

James interjected. "I don't know, Anoki. We were going over to Carlos's so Nita could break up with him, but now she doesn't know what to do."

Anoki and Orlana looked at me as though I had lost my mind (which I had). Orlana continued staring at me in amazement while Anoki walked over to me, sat next to me on the couch, and lovingly said, "Okay, Muchacha, this is your big break. You have the strength of your friends to rely on if you feel weak. This is your chance to make it right."

Do you know what? Thank God for James and Anoki. This was the moment when I became strong. I'm not sure where the burst of energy came from, but I got up from the couch and blurted out, "Let's do this."

Anoki grinned and congratulated me on my brave decision. Then he said, "Take care of my sister, you guys. Well, Orlana and me are on our way to see *Zombies Return*. See you guys later." As Anoki walked out of the house like a zombie, Orlana closed the door behind them, saying, "You can do it, Nita. Bye, everybody!"

We started to leave for Carlos's house, but before we were even out the door, my cell phone rang. I looked to see who it was. I couldn't believe it! I just looked at the phone with a blank stare.

"Is it that fool?" Mercedes asked.

All I could do was look at her.

Can It Be Different This Time?

My crew was freaked out by my blank stare. "Ain't this something?" Luisa said angrily. "You might as well answer it, Morena. We'll wait for you down here."

I went to my room to take the call. Feeling slightly frightened way, I said, "Hey, Carlos."

His tone was very loving. "Hey, babe. I was wondering if I could take you to dinner this evening. Maybe we could go to that new Spanish restaurant, Con Amores. I think it would be romantic."

Excuse me? I'm about to break up with this fool, and he says that?

"I'm sorry that I've been a jerk," he continued. "Can I pick you up? My mom is lending me her car."

Oh brother! My knees actually got weak when Carlos said that. I had no idea what to say, but I said something that I lived to regret. Yep, you guessed it: "Sure. You can pick me up." Carlos was on his way.

Let me play it safe by assuming you think I'm an idiot.

The hardest part was telling my friends what I had done. They had done so much for me, and I didn't want to let them down. I had to be honest and tell them the truth. As soon as I went downstairs to the living room where my friends were, Luisa cried out, "So … you told him we were coming, right?"

James saw in my face that it was a different story. "I think there's been a change in plans. Nita, what is it?"

I didn't want to say, but I had to. "He invited me out to dinner. I have to at least give him a chance."

Let me tell you how the rest of that "wonderful" conversation went:

JAMES: What? Nita … what?

MERCEDES: Oh lord, I knew it! I knew this was going to happen. That bitch got to you.

ALICIA: Nita, I thought you were sure this time.

LUISA: Morena, what did Carlos say?

ME: He wants to take me out to dinner. I have to at least hear him out.

MERCEDES: No you don't! Who does he think he is, anyway?

JAMES: Nita, you were so sure. What happened?

MERCEDES: He got in her head. That's what guys do. I hate Carlos.

LUISA: I don't believe any of this. Carlos is never going to change. I don't care what he says or does for you. He will continue to hurt you.

JAMES: That's right, girl. There's no changing a trifling man. So I guess our job is done here.

LUISA: I can't take much more of this. Morena, we'll see you tomorrow.

ALICIA: Wait, Luisa. Nita (*looking at me with sad eyes*), I know you're scared or at least worried. None of us knows what it's like to be in your situation. So if you need time to figure this out, we'll give you all the time you need. Right, everybody?

JAMES: Damn … okay. Fine.

LUISA: Look …

ALICIA: Luisa.

LUISA: Okay, okay. Fine.

MERCEDES: That dumbass Car— … okay.
We'll give you time, Nita.

ME: Thanks everybody. I didn't know it
would be this hard.

ALICIA: We love you, girl. (*We do a
group hug.*)

My crew left to go home, and I waited for Carlos.
Twenty minutes passed when I thought it would only be
five minutes. *So he asks me out, but then he takes forever
to come?* My doorbell finally rang. It was Carlos, but how I
wished it had been Devante. I walked out, locking the front
door behind me since my parents were still in church and
Anoki and Orlana were at the movies. Carlos took me by the
hand and escorted me to the passenger side of his mother's
car—I think it was a Toyota Camry—and we headed to Con
Amores for dinner.

The place was really beautiful, but I couldn't stop
thinking about Devante. To be honest, I thought about my
friends and family also. They had all thought I was ready to
break up with Carlos. How could I have let them all down?
What was I doing with him, anyway? I wanted to leave, but
it was better to at least hear what he had to say.

Carlos had a way of making me feel like he was
being sincere, when in reality, he was thinking of ways to
manipulate me. He was skilled at hurting people. I'm just
sorry that I didn't realize any of this sooner.

We were seated at a lovely table by the window, with a view overlooking a park. "You look beautiful, Nita," he said. Yeah, I'd had on jeans, a T-shirt, and sneakers, but I changed into a black skirt and white blouse with black shoes for dinner.

I looked him the eyes and said, "Thank you. So what are we celebrating?" Carlos and I had never gone to a restaurant like Con Amores before. What was he up to?

This is what we talked about:

> CARLOS: I just wanted to take you somewhere
>   nice.

> ME: It's just that you've never brought me
>   to a place like this before.

> CARLOS: Well I just got a new job. Now I can
>   take you wherever you wanna go.

> ME: That's all good … but I really … What
>   is your new job? (*I'm now in gentle
>   panic mode*.)

> CARLOS: Well, my boy Juan hooked me up
>   with a connection. He said we'd be
>   bringing in tons of money! (*It didn't
>   take a genius to know what Carlos was
>   talking about. Seriously? Selling weed
>   was his big job?*)

ME: (*Come to think of it, I wasn't shocked at all at the news.*) Carlos, what in the world is going on? You think I'm stupid or something? Why weed? What about your mother ... or Tinequa? Your mother will throw you out for sure.

CARLOS: My mother will never find out.

Me: Yeah, until the cops come looking for you again. At least think about your daughter. What if you end up in jail because of this crazy job?

CARLOS: Look Nita, stop worrying about me. Everything will work out fine.

ME, *waiting until the waitress has set down our lemonades.* Carlos, we need ... (*I'm trying to work up the courage to tell him how I feel.*)

CARLOS: Yes. Stop worrying. I love you.

ME: (*I don't know what happened, but I thought about my life and ...*) Do you? Or do you even know what love is? You say you love me, but you are blind. (*Now I'm talking with more assurance.*)

> Love isn't hitting. I don't like the way
> things are.
>
> CARLOS: Babe, I'm sorry. I've been under
> a lot pressure lately. I don't know …
> school is crazy, trying to raise
> Tinequa … I don't know. I love you,
> Nita. I'm trying to make things right.

I say nothing; I feel lost. We order our food.

I couldn't even talk about us after he told me what he was going through. Yes, I know. That should have been the day to break up with Carlos. Well, I just hoped my friends would still be ready when I needed them again. I felt trapped in my relationship—and if I felt that way, the decision to leave should've been easy for me. I needed to get away from Carlos, and I needed to do it fast.

When Monday finally came, I went to school feeling confident. My confidence was premature, because I still hadn't broken up with Carlos, but I think it came from everyone supporting me. I didn't know how to approach Carlos; that's why I needed the help of my friends.

Well, as it happened, when I got to my locker, my crew was right there waiting for me. I was actually glad to see them after that drama with Carlos the night before. My friends were standing in front of my locker with their arms folded. Even James was there. He said with his arms still folded, "Hey girl. We are here because we've made a decision. We are going to break up with Carlos for you. We know that you didn't do it last night, because you didn't call anyone."

I had a feeling that's what was going on—they were tired of me changing my mind about Carlos. I guess they had a right to be annoyed with me, but no one was madder at me than myself.

Now Mercedes was the only one with her arms still folded. She said she was going to do the breakup for me, but I convinced all of them that I would do it. They wanted it done that same day. Well, that was something that I needed to think about. After we talked awhile, I told them, "When I'm ready, I will let y'all know." They gave me a group hug, and the first-period bell rang.

My first class was English, my favorite subject, so it was easy to breeze through it. The next period I had a scheduled appointment with Mrs. Gandolfini. As soon as I entered her office, she started smiling. I sat in the chair on the other side of her desk, feeling really happy. This was our conversation:

> MRS. GANDOLFINI: Hello, Denita. So how are you feeling today? You look fantastic.

> ME: Hello, Mrs. Gandolfini. For some reason I feel very confident.

> MRS. GANDOLFINI: That's good. Does that confidence have anything to do with Carlos? If it does, that's okay. Do you

think you are ready to do this today?
It's okay not to be sure.

ME: Maybe it was a long time coming.
Maybe Carlos isn't the right guy for me.
Maybe this should be the day. What do
you think, Mrs. Gandolfini?

MRS. GANDOLFINI: It's all up to you, Denita.
You can do whatever works best for
you. It's okay to wait until the timing is
right for you. Only you can make that
decision.

I knew Mrs. Gandolfini was right. I knew it was now
or never with Carlos. So what was really bothering me?
Maybe I just didn't want to lose him. Maybe I thought that
he would hurt me if he knew how I really felt. On the other
hand, I would look like a failure if I didn't go through with
the breakup. I was definitely in the hot seat now.

So what was I supposed to do? The answer was simple:
get the crew. They'd know what to do.

I texted Mercedes and rest of the crew, including James,
asking them to meet me after school at the pizza shop. This
breakup was going to take place whether I wanted it to
happen or not. After eighth period, the last one of the day,
I met with Carlos in front of my locker and we headed to
the pizza shop together. As we walked, he seemed very
different—more … I guess … loving? … than he had been

in a long time. So this was the guy I wanted to break up with? Was this the right time? I really didn't know what to do.

When we arrived at the pizza shop at around three thirty, I saw my crew in a booth at the back corner, engaged in conversation. I could only imagine what they were talking about. They were probably talking about me and how I couldn't make up my mind about Carlos. All I needed them to do was be on standby in case I needed them. I wasn't sure how things would go with Carlos—he had too many mood swings.

We sat down in a booth, and I said to Carlos, "Why does it seem like you have so many mood swings with me? I doubt you act that way around your friends." I don't think that he was ready for that one. I guess I couldn't help myself. I needed to let him know how I was feeling about him.

"Babe, I just been under a lot of pressure these days. The police said they're watching me, so I guess I have to be on my best behavior. I'm doing my best to take care of Tinequa as well. There's so much going on in my life. Things between us can be good, but there are some things that can't change."

Then things got weird. Here we go:

> CARLOS: Come on, babe. You know that I
> love you.

> ME: I don't think you even understand love.
> Okay, what's that job you have? Selling
> weed? You say you love me, right?

Maybe that's one way to prove your
loyalty to me: stop selling weed!

CARLOS: Babe, if I didn't have a daughter,
I would stop. My mom doesn't know
what I do, but she knows that I'm
making money. She told me that I
needed to do something to take care of
my daughter. I guess because of school,
I chose to sell weed. You may not agree
with my choice, but damn it, it's what
I have to do.

ME, *using my sincere voice.* What about
your mom? What do you think she'll
say if she finds out the truth about
your job?

CARLOS: Well … let's hope she won't be too
mad. Let's face it, babe—if she really
cared about what I did, wouldn't she
have asked me? She doesn't care as long
as I'm bringing home money.

That conversation left me speechless. Maybe Carlos had
changed. In a way, I'd grown to have a lot of respect for him.
I thought it was my fear because of the pending breakup, but
it wasn't even that; my respect for him was genuine. He was

doing it all at such a young age. We were seventeen years old now, and he had a lot on his plate.

After Carlos and I finished our slices, he checked his phone and told me that he'd received a text from a customer and needed to leave for the South Side. He kissed me and left.

With Carlos gone, my crew immediately came over to my booth. Mercedes looked me square in the face and screeched, "What happened, girl? We saw that Carlos left in a hurry. What'd you say to him?"

"Carlos had a customer," I said calmly. "I didn't break up with him. I couldn't. Carlos has changed, y'all."

James nodded. "Yeah, he has. I saw him when I was looking for something in my locker. We started talking about his daughter. What the hell is going on?"

What the hell was going on was that Carlos had gotten a glimpse of reality. When he found out that Rhonda wasn't coming back to the States, he probably panicked. Remember Rhonda, Carlos's baby mama who'd decided to stay in the Dominican Republic with her family? She was nice, but she and Carlos had agreed that he would be responsible for raising Tinequa. For a seventeen-year-old, Carlos really had his act together, in a weird way.

As I knew they would be, my friends were undecided how they felt about Carlos. Of course, Mercedes said, "Well I still don't like Carlos. I think you need to dump his ass, and he is still a dumb bitch. Now, what are you gonna do, girl?" Luisa had had enough and decided to stay out of it for a minute. Alicia said, "Nita, really? I can't believe this. Did you not hear it when we said that Carlos will never change? I know what it looks like right now, but Carlos needs to stop and realize what he's doing to you. He has you confused." James added, "Girl, he's a mess. He may have changed, but who's to say that he won't go back to the old ways? You understand, Nita?"

I told James that I understood, but did I? Not really. My parents had taught me that people can change, so I felt I should believe that Carlos could change too. *Should I listen to my friends or listen to my heart?* I wondered.

When I got home that evening, Luisa called me and shouted at me. "Morena, wake up! What is wrong with you? Carlos is using you! Can't you see that? The crew and I have been talking, and we think that it's pathetic what Carlos is putting you through. We are there for you any time you need us, but you can't be blinded by his changing ways. Get a grip, girl!" Luisa was very harsh, but she wasn't wrong. I assured her that I was working on the breakup.

I guess Luisa was right: I had been blinded by Carlos's changed ways. She told me it was best for me to stay away from Carlos until I was ready to break up with him, since being around him was so hard for me. I decided that she was absolutely correct. Staying away from Carlos was going to be hard, but I had to do it to make myself stronger.

Later that evening, I was coming up the stairs from dinner when I heard my phone ring. Guess who? That's right, it was Devante! Of all the people I knew who could have been calling, it had to be Devante. Needless to say, I didn't want to talk with Carlos, because I hadn't broken up with him yet. Devante would probably ask countless questions about Carlos and me. What was I going to say? Well, here's what happened:

ME: Hey, Devante. What's going on?

DEVANTE: Well, I called because I was thinking about you. I was thinking about you and Carlos, and how you should let me help you.

ME: Look, Devante …

DEVANTE: Nita, I didn't call to lecture you. You have a lot to deal with. I don't want to confuse things, because you probably get hassled by your friends and family about Carlos all the time. I just wish that you wouldn't shut me out. I care too much about you to just let you go. Let me help you, babe.

ME: (*Wow, he called me babe, and I just melted.*) Devante, you are way too good to me. Thank you. Can you just be there for me when I need a shoulder to lean on? I promise to break up with

Carlos soon. I don't understand why it's
so hard for me, but it is. I will do it. I
promise.

DEVANTE: Okay. I'm here for you, Nita.

I was losing my mind. There was a hot dude waiting
for me to break up with Carlos, but I couldn't get away
from him.

Devante and I talked on the phone all night. He said that
I was way too smart to be Carlos's girlfriend, and that he'd
been wondering how we ended up together anyway. To be
honest, I was wondering the same thing.

Carlos had my world spinning. I needed to let him go.

What Is My Heart Saying?

My parents always told me that my teenage years were supposed to be simple. Well, I really didn't think so. Who were they talking about, anyway? Those girls on TV? My life was full of surprises. When Carlos and I first got together, I was sure that our relationship would always be great. I never once thought he would put his hands on me. Was Carlos a bad person? Maybe not. It was obvious that he had some issues, but we usually had a good time together. In fact, he was usually a gentleman. So what happened? Were there warning signs? If there were, why hadn't I noticed them? What could've made Carlos a better guy for me? Did he realize what he was doing wrong? All those questions made me wonder if there was something wrong with me.

When I woke up Saturday morning, my sister was packing to go on a weekend trip with her boyfriend. I didn't want to bother her because she looked so busy, but I really needed advice. I walked up to her and said, "Orlana, what's wrong with me? Why can't I break up with Carlos? I know he's changed, but won't I be a fool if I stay with him?" I put my face in my hands and started to cry.

I sat down on Orlana's bed, and she sat down next to me with her arm around my shoulder and replied, "Nita, are you crazy? There's nothing wrong with you. I'm not sure why you can't break up with Carlos. Maybe it's because you love him so much. One thing that Mom and Dad taught us is that love is simple. There shouldn't be one million reasons why you love someone. Carlos probably loves you too, but his love is different. He shows it by hurting you. In reality, that's not love, but Carlos may not realize that. You and your friends will figure something out. We're all rooting for you to do the right thing."

My sister was right—love was simple. Carlos made it hard for me to love him. I put all my energy into loving him, only to feel pain in the end. Was that wrong? I loved Carlos, but at what cost? What did he have to do for me to see him for who he really was? Devante was a gentleman; he hadn't forced me to decide between him and Carlos. Still, I felt I owed it to myself to be honest with Devante and Carlos. Why did I need so much help with this situation?

Mercedes made it sound so simple to just break up with Carlos, but it was the hardest thing in the world. On the one hand, I didn't want him to blame me. On the other hand, I didn't want to feel like I wasn't giving him a chance to show me that he'd changed. Where was my place in this decision?

When Wednesday finally arrived, I had a new attitude. I was ready to face the world. Carlos was on my mind, but not in the way that you might think. I was trying to figure out how I was going to break up with him. As I stood in front of the mirror in our downstairs bathroom, brushing my hair, I thought of nice ways to end things with Carlos. Did he really deserve "nice"? Maybe not, but my parents had taught us to always have respect. After all, Carlos was a person, and I guess he deserved respect like anyone else. I went to school happy, but I felt a little lost.

When I arrived, my crew was waiting for me and James to join them before we went to first period. I saw James flying to us from down the hallway. I needed to understand the urgency of this meeting in front of my locker. So I asked Mercedes (since she looked like she had something to say), "Girl what is it?"

Mercedes hugged me and said excitedly, "Devante told me that he will wait for you, girl. Do you know what that means? That means that you *have* to break up with Carlos. Carlos is in the way of you and Devante. So if you don't hurry up and break up with him, I will be forced to kick his ass."

Luisa gave a Mercedes confused look and said to me, "Anyway, Morena, you already know what to do. Just do it already!"

James had no sympathy at all. "It's now or never, girl. Either you break up with Carlos or I will have to join Mercedes in a good, old-fashioned ass whupping." James and Mercedes slapped five on that one.

Alicia, who was usually the sweet one with an encouraging word, had absolutely nothing to say. She just hugged me.

Talk about pressure. My crew, I guess, was tired of me stalling with Carlos. They had no idea what I was going through. Carlos was someone I had grown to love. It was hard to break up with him because of what we had. He had been nice, once upon a time, and I missed that. Maybe I thought I could change him. Maybe there was a part of me that knew he wanted to be a good person.

Well, I guess it wasn't up to me to fix Carlos. Mrs. Gandolfini had told me that we have to know when we've had enough. Now, my friends, I had had enough.

That night at around eight thirty, I received a call from Alan. He told me that he had the best surprise in the world for me. Well, he *was* going to surprise me, but I pushed him enough that he finally put an end to my suspense. He told me that he and his family were going to be visiting some relatives in Chicago—they'd be in town for a week—and he wanted to spend some time together. I thought the timing was perfect.

That Saturday, Dad and Anoki picked up Alan from his aunt's house. I was happy to see Alan, since the last time I'd seen him I was fifteen years old. It was a good time to catch up on things. I wasn't going to forget about my responsibility to break up with Carlos, and I thought maybe Alan would be the motivation I needed to help me.

When he walked in the door with my family, I was excited to see my buddy. I hugged him so tight he had the nerve to say, "Nita, if you don't let go, I'm pretty sure you'll break something." We all had a huge laugh after that. The whole family got together that night to watch a scary movie called *This Zombie Just Won't Die*. I guess it was supposed to be one of those funny scary movies. Anyway, after the movie ended, Alan and our family started reminiscing about life back in Oregon. He was doing well in school, and so was I. Our families were proud of us. So why did I feel empty inside?

That night, Alan slept over at my house. He stayed in a sleeping bag on the floor of my room. Before you start thinking nasty thoughts about me, Alan stayed in the sleeping bag *the whole night*. Besides, my mom made us keep my bedroom door open. (My mom did not play that!) I couldn't sleep, so I decided to write in my diary. When I was done, I just sat there, staring out the window.

I must have been sitting and staring for a while before Alan finally sat up and said, "Nita, what's wrong? And don't say it's nothing, because I know it probably has to do with Carlos. Spit it out."

How could I keep this information from my best childhood friend in the whole world? This was our conversation:

> ME: Alan, I don't understand how things got so bad for me. Carlos is someone I have grown to love. When he hurt me, it broke my heart. No one understands the pressure I'm going through. I care about Carlos. I know that it's not right to be with him, but how can I just turn off my feelings?

ALAN: I don't think turning off your feelings
  for Carlos will change things, because
  feelings can always return. You've
  already grasped that Carlos is no good
  for you. Now you just have to strategize
  your next step. You don't know this,
  but my mom knew a girl in her high
  school back in Barbados that was also
  hurt by her boyfriend several times.
  The last time he beat her, it was with a
  tire iron. He thought she was cheating
  on him. My mom watched the news that
  evening and saw her friend's face on
  the screen. The news reporter said that
  her friend's face was smashed in—her
  boyfriend had killed her. My sister and
  I still talk about that gruesome story.
  My mom only shared it with us because
  I told her that I was concerned about
  your situation.

ME: That is so terrible, Al. I don't want
  what happened to your mom's friend to
  happen to me.

ALAN: I'm here for you, Nita. You've got
  to be strong. You know what's right. I
  know it's hard, but Carlos needs to find

his own way without you. He obviously
needs help.

That conversation with Alan opened my eyes to what was really going on. I was only thinking of my own needs, which were valid, but Carlos also needed help. I was not what he needed. Maybe he needed anger management, or even a counselor. Maybe he needed both. Carlos was an okay dude, but he was toxic. What Alan was talking about was something I never had to deal with, since my childhood was different from Carlos's. He was broken. Janet once told me that Carlos's father split after his third birthday. He lived with his mother and one of his mother's boyfriends. Carlos never talked about any of that stuff with me before—I guess he was too proud. I grew to understand that you really don't know a person until you ask enough questions.

Well, I was grateful—not just for Alan, but for the wisdom that he shared with me. I now realized why it was hard to break up with Carlos. All along, I'd just been thinking about myself and how I needed to get out of the relationship. I never thought about the fact that I wasn't the only one who needed help. Carlos always gave the impression that everything was okay, and then when things didn't go his way, he blamed the world. I still didn't understand a lot about what he was about, but I was sure that someday I would figure it out.

Alan and I spent that Saturday at the mall with the crew. Mercedes loved Alan. She kept calling him her "boo thang." Alan didn't care. He thought Mercedes was cute anyway.

Mercedes couldn't help saying to Alan, "So when are we gonna settle down and just do the damn thing? Forget these fools." Okay, clearly she had lost her mind then, but we all laughed it off. We knew Mercedes was nuts. Anyway, everyone loved Alan, James too. Yes, James loved Alan. You know about James, so don't act surprised, people.

While we were at the mall, the focus was on Alan and not all on me. The gang kept asking him questions like they'd never met anyone in their lives. Then, for some crazy reason, James shouted out, "Oh goodness! Why are we forgetting the hot topic of the day? I don't want to have to stab Carlos in his sleep!"

What was wrong with James? He knew what a hard time I was having with this mess. Couldn't they have offered me some help with my problem? Was it a problem, though? Maybe it was. How would that look, anyway? James would not harm a fly, and he knew how much I loved Carlos.

"Girl, what is going on?" he said to me. "We've avoided talking about Carlos because we knew you needed time. But this is taking too long. You know that Carlos is no good for you. Alan even said that. Isn't that right, Alan?"

Of course Alan didn't say anything. I really needed him to say something, but Mercedes jumped in, as usual. "I know what you're saying, James. Carlos is never going to leave the picture as long as she doesn't do anything. Nita may never rid us of this terrible tragedy."

Did they really need to say those things? *I guess I'm alone in this,* I thought.

Luisa had been quiet so far, but now she couldn't help herself. "I'm definitely not getting involved again. Nita thinks we're playing with her, but I'm not playing. Carlos is a jerk, Carlos is an idiot, and I really can't stand him. So if Nita wants to mess around with him, who am I to say anything?"

I looked at Luisa with embarrassment. I knew I needed to do better. I didn't know what it was going to take for me to be rid of Carlos. Actually, I did know.

Our day at the mall was fun for me and the gang. I just wished Alan could have stayed in Chicago a little longer, but he had to go back with his family the next week, so I knew if I wanted to do something, I had to do it fast. I also knew that Alan would bug me the whole time he was in Chicago, so I needed to think about that.

I decided that it would be a good idea to invite Carlos over for a chat, or maybe we could go out on another date and I could talk to him then. But would I make any more progress this time? I didn't know.

When we finally got home from the mall, I decided to call Carlos while the gang was still at my the house. By that time everyone was home—my whole family as well as my friends. We all met in the living room since there was room for everyone. I put Carlos on speaker on my iPhone so that everyone could hear when I spoke to him. My friends did make me stronger, so I felt I should use them while I could. After all, my parents had told me that my friends would be a good asset to help me with Carlos. That Sunday at the mall was unforgettable. To this day I still remember what Alan told me. I wanted to start making changes when Monday came. The advice my guidance counselor had given me was very good. She only wanted what was best for me, as my family did.

Still, I felt lost, and I thought no one else could understand what I was going through. At the last minute, I decided that I wasn't ready to call Carlos. Maybe I was losing it. Maybe I just needed a little more advice. Actually, I didn't need any more advice, because the advice I had already received was perfect. I just needed motivation. That's what was keeping me from doing the job.

Being in high school is hard. You think you know what you're doing, and then you don't know what you're doing. There are so many twists and turns. Well, something had to be done, and it had to be done now.

Alan stayed at my house while I went to school. He had to stay behind so he could travel with his parents during the week. On Monday I walked to school with my friends, as usual, and as we were approaching the building, we ran into Carlos. He looked at me with those wonderful hazel eyes and said, "Nita, what's good? I was thinking about you yesterday. What was going on?"

I didn't want to answer him, because I knew the gang would be mad. I did answer though. "I was just hanging out with the gang. I wanted them to get to know Alan. Maybe you should come by so you can meet him also."

He gave Mercedes a weird look and said, "Yeah, babe. I'll come by later to meet Alan. See you at school, babe." Then he kissed me on the cheek.

That moment was so intense! Goodness gracious, Mercedes—she was so scary! Wow, I have to admit, that was more funny than scary to me.

Anyway, as soon as I got to school, I stopped by Mrs. Gandolfini's office. I just needed to hear her say to me that I was doing the right thing. I felt that Carlos and I were making progress, but it was too little, too late. I also thought me and my friends were tired of the situation, and what was I getting out of it, anyway?

During school, Alan kept texting me: "Did you do it? Did you do it? Did you do it?" Just like that. Why did he have to say it three times? Alan was silly. He was right, though. What was taking me so long?

Will Everyone Still Love Me?

Last week had been so hard for me. I kept thinking, *What should I do now?* There are so many problems you face—which I didn't know about, of course—when you're breaking up with someone. Being a teen is supposed to be fun, and it's no fun breaking up with the man that you love. Okay, so he wasn't a man—I just really loved him. Carlos was a wonderful guy, and I thought if everyone gave him a chance, they would know that too. So what if he had problems? So what if I couldn't understand him right now? I just knew that I really loved him and he loved me.

Ending things with Carlos would probably complicate things. I don't like complications. My family would probably understand, since they knew I always made the right decisions, so I guessed that I should tell them exactly what I was thinking. But what *was* I thinking? I was about to go back to a dude no one seemed to like—though that also could have been my fault.

Alan did give me some good advice, though. He knew I'd do the right thing as well. Goodness gracious! This wasn't getting any easier. Well, I had to face the music. I didn't like this at all. This was way too hard for me, being so young and in high school. I should have been worrying about cheerleading practice or the high school musical or eating in the cafeteria, something cool like that. But Mom did say love was simple, so I'll just go with that.

Although I was glad it was finally Monday, I'd been sad to see Alan go home Saturday. He was such a great friend to me, and I was happy that all my friends had gotten to know him. Mercedes still jokes that he's her boyfriend, even if Alan may or may not be looking for girlfriend right now.

Alan was always the guy that got the girl but didn't want the girl. No, no, no … he's not gay. He just really likes to look. He'd had girlfriends, but it took him a long time to realize who he wanted to be with. I guess that's what being in high school is really all about: you're always looking. Of course, Mercedes wanted Alan's phone number and so I gave it to her, and after that they talked all the time. She was a bit loud, and she loved her wonderful curse words, but I thought they could make it work.

So now there was just me. Mercedes and Alan had a bright future, but what about me?

I kept thinking, *If I stay with Carlos, everyone will hate me. If I don't end up with Carlos, I will hate myself.* I figured that he just needed a chance to make it work. I was the kind of girl who had lots of patience, and I thought we could work together on this one. Yes, he had a daughter—nobody liked that. Plus I'd talked to everyone, and everyone knew that I was going to break up with Carlos, so when I changed my mind, it was weird. Where was Alan when I needed him?

After school that Monday, I was so happy to see Luisa across the street at the pizza shop, ordering her slice. She was speaking in Spanish to a really cute guy. I thought I'd seen him before, although I wasn't sure of his name. (To be honest, I still don't remember his name.) I crossed the street, walked up to Luisa, and gave her a huge hug, saying, "Girl, I really missed you!"

Luisa smiled at me and said, "Nita, I've been thinking about you all weekend. What's going on? Are you going to do it or not?" Let me break down how that conversation went after we sat down:

ME: Is that all you have to say to me?

LUISA, *smiling at me like a sister.* Of course not, girl! You know I love you.

ME: I was just surprised that that was all you had to say to me. Well, I have been having some problems. Of course, you know what problem I'm talking about, right?

LUISA: Maybe I do or maybe I don't. That's for you to tell me. It's weird that we're talking about this when you know what you need to do. Are you scared again? Nita! What is happening now? Carlos is no good! What is it going to take?

ME: I don't know. I know I love Carlos. I can't leave him. He has too much going on. What will he do without me? I don't want to know the answer to that.

LUISA: I'm done. We've talked to you, and your family has talked to you. (*She's getting more and more upset.*) I really don't know what's happening to you. I get that you're scared, but Carlos isn't worth it. What about Devante? You know Devante loves you, girl.

ME: I know, I know. Look, Luisa, I have to follow my heart. Everyone will understand that. Don't do this to me— and please don't tell Mercedes. She would never let me forget it, and I will never forget it if she talked to me about anything dealing with Carlos. I have enough to worry about.

LUISA: Okay. I'm done, and I mean that. I will love you and be your friend. I will always be your best friend. Just don't ask me to like Carlos with his dumb ass. I don't get this guy. What has he done for you, anyway?

ME: I don't understand why you can't like Carlos. He has done a lot for me. He's a wonderful guy. I just really wish my friends would love him just the way I do. My family doesn't like him, I know you guys don't like him, and I know Alan hates him just because of what I've said about him. I just want everyone to leave me alone and understand that I love Carlos with all my heart. Maybe I'm too young to understand love. But I do know one thing: I love Carlos. I wanted to talk to you because I wanted to get your opinion about what I should do. I see now that that was a mistake. You will never like Carlos, and I am done asking you to I love him, and I do want to be friends. I just don't want to ask your opinion about Carlos anymore. We can move on to new things and talk about our lives the way we've always done.

LUISA: Okay, girl. Nita, I will always protect you. All of us feel the same way. I wasn't going to tell you this, but Anoki called me the other day. He is worried about you, and so is Orlana. If your parents knew what you wanted to do,

they would flip their lids; however, you
are my best friend. So if you want me
not to tell anyone, I won't. Just don't ask
me to like some dumb stupid jackass
bitch. I can't stand that dummy.

ME: Wow, Luisa. That was really harsh, but
I think I understand. So let's talk about
something else.

That conversation was crazy. There was no liking
Carlos for Luisa. I guess it's safe to say that Mercedes felt
the same way, and I wasn't going to beg her to like him
either. Mercedes and Luisa had their minds made up. I don't
think Alicia cared much one way or the other—she usually
loved anyone we loved. James, on the other hand, didn't
like a lot of people. He definitely couldn't stand Carlos. He
would always ask me, "How's Mr. Dumbass?" I would just
look at him and answer with some interesting comment. I
read somewhere—who knows who said it—that you're not
always gonna like everything everyone does, and it's up to
you to decide if you want to understand it or not. All I know
is that at the time, I thought I was doing the right thing by
staying with Carlos. I guess we all learn.

After I did my homework that night, I was happy to get
a call from Mercedes. We talked for several minutes, and
then she brought up the one thing she could've left alone: she
asked me about Carlos. Mercedes never mixed words, so I
just humored her. Whatever she asked me I just answered.

I have to admit, though, it was hard to explain what was going on with Carlos. I didn't want to tell her that I wasn't breaking up with him.

The fact is, I didn't get to talk to Carlos because he was taking tests all day. That week was makeup exams for everyone who had missed Regents week, which he had, so he had to buckle down. Anyway, Mercedes was such a crazy girl. Why couldn't she just accept the fact that I didn't want to talk about Carlos? It was not easy getting her to leave me alone about it. So I just answered her the best way I could without giving anything away. When she finally got around to the big question ("Did you break up with him or not?") I didn't want to tell her anything, because I knew she would hate me for it. I'm glad Luisa kept her promise. She's a real good friend.

There is no need to talk about what Mercedes and I said on the phone, because it wasn't important. I simply told her what she wanted to know, and I didn't say anything else. I never once mentioned that Carlos and I were done— that would have made her day. But she didn't know that Carlos and I were still seeing each other either. Mercedes had always been like my younger sister, even though she was only two months younger than me, and I wanted to ease her mind for the time being, so I simply told her, "I'll deal with it." She seemed to be okay with that. I didn't want to give away too much. The truth was, I didn't think anyone was okay with me not giving away all the information they thought they needed.

This year had been a crazy one. I had my friends on one side telling me what to do, and then I had my family on the other side telling me what to do. The truth was, I really didn't know what to do, but I knew I was going to stay with Carlos. That's where my heart was, and that's where I needed to stay. Carlos wasn't a bad guy. People just needed to get to know him like I did—or like I thought I did. I have to admit, Carlos did change over time; however, he had his good days and his bad days, and everyone has those. So what if he had a child in high school? I'm sure everyone had some kind of problem.

The question remained, though: what about Devante? Did I love him? Of course I did. Did I want to be with him? Of course I did. But the timing was way off. I just wished I had it in my mind to leave Carlos. I just didn't think it was right. I really loved Carlos. I know he wasn't the best guy, but I wanted to be with him. Still, Devante was everything that I wanted in a guy.

I needed a break—this was so crazy. I knew I needed to be with someone decent, and in my mind at the time, Carlos was decent. If no one else thought that—okay, fine. There would always be someone who didn't like who you were with. I just wished my family and friends could see what I saw. To this day, they still can't believe me and Carlos had a thing. Well, we did. High school was a crazy place.

To be honest, the fact that I couldn't bring myself to break up with Carlos wasn't his fault. It's just that I never wanted to hurt him—I loved him so much. I wished I didn't love him, but I did, even though I knew it was wrong. Was Carlos the innocent victim in all this, or was I? I decided to deal with the facts anyway. If my friends said something, I'd just tell them, "I'll deal with it."

As the weekend slowly crept up on me, I knew I would be getting pressure from everyone. What was I going to tell them about Carlos this time? I hadn't known what to tell them the time before. Friday evening around six, Carlos called me at my house. He said he wanted to hang out and have a good time with me. I wanted to go because I loved him, so I figured, *Why not?* It was funny, because at the same time, Mercedes called me too. She wanted to know if I wanted to go see *Dead Man*. What was it about scary movies and this crew?

Well, I decided to go out with Carlos, and Mercedes was furious with me. I couldn't blame her, but Carlos was my boyfriend—and why did I need to make a choice? Anyway, that's what I thought then. Mercedes said a curse word that begins with an *f,* which I do not say, and I decided to just let her have that one. I didn't argue with her. After all, she was one of my best friends. She got off the phone a little angry, but she didn't want to make a fight with me either.

Of course Carlos was happy. I was happy too. I was getting ready for our date when I heard a knock at the door. I ran downstairs and saw Mercedes standing at the door, smiling. That was really funny, but I hadn't expected her to come. When I opened the door, she said, "Where are you going, girl?" We talked for about five minutes, but I don't think she got the message. When I told her that I was going out with Carlos, she freaked out. Mercedes had forgotten that I had just told her that I was going out with Carlos that night. I knew she cared about me, so I usually let things slide when she yelled at me like a maniac.

As I left the house, Mercedes stared at me with a weird look. She always had a weird look when I said something she didn't like—Luisa did the same thing. Alicia didn't worry about it too much, because she knew that I would eventually make the right decision. That's how my mom was too. My dad was a different story, and I guess Anoki and Alana were kind of like him. Me getting everyone to love Carlos was just not happening anyway, so I decided to move on.

I met Carlos at Calvin's Steakhouse. I wasn't sure what he wanted to talk about, but I knew he wanted to be alone. That's how it always was with Carlos. We never really hung out with his friends and my friends together, because my friends couldn't stand him. In a perfect world, everyone would have gotten along and I would have been happy. My world wasn't like that, and I had to figure out that I was alone in this one. That's not a good thing, but what was I supposed to do?

Now the question remained: what about Devante? He was everything everyone wanted for me—and I wanted the same thing. Carlos was the only thing in the way. My feelings hadn't changed for Devante; I just didn't know it. Now that I look back, I can see that it is hard to be a teenager.

You never know what you want, but everyone else seems to. There is no guide for how to be a teenager. You just have to go with the flow and hope you learn along the way. So Devante was in my life, but not in the way I needed him to be. I wanted him to be closer, like a boyfriend, and he couldn't be my boyfriend because of Carlos. Carlos liked Devante, but he knew I liked Devante too.

At the steakhouse, Carlos was a gentleman. I knew he would be, because he had changed tremendously—it was almost surreal. I didn't know if he was going to change again, so I just enjoyed the moment. While we were at dinner, I received a text message, and guess who it was? You guessed it—it was Devante. "What's up?"

Of course I didn't answer, because I was with Carlos. I knew he would get suspicious, so I left it alone. After we left the steakhouse and I was in the car with Carlos, I thought about answering Devante's text. If I answered and said it was Mercedes or Luisa or Alicia or someone else other than Devante, Carlos would flip his lid. He would start asking, "Who's that, babe?" I didn't feel like going through that whole thing.

He always did that: whenever someone would text me or call me, he had to know it all. I didn't like arguing with Carlos. No one liked arguing with Carlos. He always got so angry. So we usually left it alone. Actually, his guy friends were the only ones who could argue with Carlos without him getting so angry.

Carlos dropped me off at my house around eight o'clock. Like I said, he was being a gentleman. To my surprise, Devante called me before I could even answer his text message. He said, "What's going on gorgeous?" It was a great conversation that ended poorly. Maybe I should tell you guys how it went that night:

> ME: Hello, handsome. I hope you're doing good.

> DEVANTE: I'm fine. I was sitting here wondering if you wanted to go out with me next weekend. Maybe we can go to the mall. I know you love your malls.

> ME: I don't know about that … I guess I have to think about it.

> DEVANTE: Why would you have to think about it? You never had to think about it before.

> ME: I know, but I'm not sure what Carlos wants to do.

> DEVANTE: Oh, so it's what Carlos needs. So now we're concerned about what Prince Carlos needs? Why do you care what that dude wants?

ME: Devante …

DEVANTE: I really don't need to hear it right
    now. All of a sudden you're concerned
    about Carlos. When was he ever
    concerned about you? I said I wasn't
    going to say anything, but I think I
    need to. Nita, you're wasting your time
    thinking Carlos can change. He has
    been that way forever.

ME: I know who Carlos is, and I know how
    he makes everybody feel. You don't
    like him, my friends don't like him—
    even my family hates him.

DEVANTE: You don't see why? I'm not going
    to speak mean of Carlos, because I
    know you love him; I just want you to
    be safe. It doesn't seem to be getting
    through to you how I feel. Maybe I
    should just leave this one alone. It's just
    that I don't want to waste my time. If
    you don't want me, I need to move on.
    You don't have to tell me to do that,
    because it's obvious that you will never
    get over Carlos. I am fighting a losing
    battle, and I hope you have a good

life. There's no sense in trying to get someone who doesn't want you.

That was it. Devante hung up the phone. I didn't want to call him back, because I felt he was angry. He had never spoken to me in that tone. He wasn't yelling at me, but he was using a voice I'd never heard before. Had I asked for that?

I was sad that whole night. I couldn't get out of my mind would Devante had said. What was I doing to myself? What was I doing to Devante? What kind of life was this? I was out of control—I couldn't stop crying. I tried to hold my mouth shut so I wouldn't make any noise. It hurt so bad. Maybe Devante was my true love and I didn't know it. Maybe Carlos was bad. I'd made a mess of things, and I did not know how to fix it. I knew Devante was gone forever if I didn't fix things.

I didn't stop crying until about midnight that night. The next day, Sunday, I just stayed home all day, crying. Now that I think about it, I really *did* cry that whole day. That afternoon, Mom knocked on my bedroom door. She opened it when she heard me quietly say, "Come in." When she walked into the room, I was on the floor, looking up at the sky through my window. I turned around to see Mom sitting on my bed.

"What's the matter, Nita?" she asked. I told her what Devante said, and she looked at me like she knew exactly what was happening. "Devante is a gentleman," she said. "I don't know why Carlos is still in your life, but you know.

You always make the right decisions. I know you'll get out of this one. I don't know how you can do it, but you always manage to do the right thing."

I told her that I was a fool. I told her that I was sorry I was such a jerk.

She said, "You're none of those things. You are my daughter. That means you will figure it out. Just make sure you stick to your guns. Carlos is not the best, but maybe you know a better way. I don't think Devante is going anywhere. He's just giving you a break. It's hard to understand guys sometimes; they don't know how to express themselves. So when they do something, you sometimes have to read between the lines. If Devante talks to you the way you say he did, it doesn't mean that he's mad at you. Don't take it personally. He's angry because he wants to be with you and you are still with Carlos. It makes him mad, but he's not mad at you. He's mad at the situation. Just remember that he still loves you and nothing has changed."

Mom was right. I felt hurt by what Devante said, but I knew he was right. And for some reason I couldn't fix it. Or was it that I didn't want to fix it? Maybe it was both. After all, I was in high school. What did I know about love with a guy? (Now I can say that; at the time I had no idea.) I didn't text or call Devante for a while. I listened to my mom.

That night I was still crying—this time because I thought I'd hurt Devante. That was not something I ever wanted to do. Carlos was my boyfriend, but Devante was my friend for life. There had to be a way out of this so that I could stop hurting people. I just decided to keep doing what I needed to do and figure out a way to end things with Carlos once and for all.

That Monday morning, I was late to school because … I was still crying. Mom knew it, but she didn't hassle me about it. She just called my homeroom teacher (she had all my teachers' numbers) to tell her that I would be a little late.

I walked to school alone that day. My friends had called earlier, offering to pick me up, but I needed to be late so that I could get myself together. Was it gonna get any easier? It never got easier. It was the hardest feeling I'd ever had to feel.

When I was walking up to the steps to my school, I saw Devante getting out of his car. I didn't say anything, but he saw me walking in and said, "How's it going?"

I was surprised that he'd said anything at all to me. "Everything is good," I said.

He gave me a slight smile, waved by, and then went to class. When you're late at my school, you have to sign a book in the attendance office. So I stopped by the office and then was off to my class.

Around fifth period, I got a text from Luisa: "Meet us in the park after school." Why did we have to meet in the park? I didn't want to meet in the park. I wanted to go home and cry my eyes out. But I did go to the park after school, and Luisa ran up to me and hugged me. Mercedes then ran up and hugged me too. Alicia hugged me a little longer, but then again she always did. Even Janet was there. She didn't hug me, but she smiled a lot. James was there too. He gave me a funny look and then started talking immediately. "So, what did you say to Devante? You know Devante and I are best friends. You know he's going to talk about you. Actually, he didn't say much."

"What did Devante say?" I asked.

"Devante loves you," he replied. "He just told me that he had a talk with you over the phone. He looked depressed about it. He didn't say much. It's just that I know my friend. He just looked different when he mentioned your name, so I knew you did something. What did you do, girl?"

What did I do to Devante? I didn't remember doing anything to Devante. I just remember telling him how I felt about my situation with Carlos. After our conversation, we hung up the phone. He was right to want to hang up. James didn't deserve to be in the confused situation of mine.

Everyone else went home, but James and I went back to my house together and sat down in the living room to do our homework. After we'd finished, James couldn't resist bringing up Devante again. This is how the conversation started:

> JAMES: What's going on with you and Devante? You know he didn't tell me why he's upset.

ME: I didn't do anything to Devante. Like I said, I just told him how I felt. Why is it a crime to be honest with someone?

JAMES: I didn't say it wasn't fine to be honest. Devante is upset and I want to know why. Did you tell him you didn't want to be with him? I know it has something to do with Carlos.

ME: I don't know what you want me to say. Carlos is my boyfriend, and I don't know what else to do about that. Devante knows how I feel, so what's the problem?

JAMES: The problem is Devante is at a loss for words. He's picking me up from your house later, so I think you need to say something to him. Look, I know you love Devante. He loves you, and if he gets upset about you and Carlos, you have to understand. He's a gentleman. He's not going to nag you like we do. Stop playing.

ME: Things are crazy, but I can deal with it.

JAMES: Can you really? Can you really deal with this? You can't even break up with Carlos. I cannot believe anything you say right now. You should've called Devante back when he hung up on you. He told me he hung up on you because he didn't know what else to say. And what else could he say? Carlos is not good, and you know that. How many times do we have to tell you? Mercedes told you a hundred times. I guess you will never leave Carlos. So what was Devante supposed to do?

ME: I know that Devante is hurt right now. It won't be for long. I do have a plan, but everyone has to give me time. It's not the way you all want it, but I have to do it this way. I don't know what else to do. Carlos is in the picture until he's not in the picture anymore.

JAMES: I guess that's it, then. So I will tell Devante that.

ME: I really didn't want this. Don't tell Devante anything. Why would you tell him anything, anyway? You're my friend too! Don't tell him anything. I'll deal with Devante. Leave it to me. This is harder than anything I've ever had to do. I will do what is right. Trust me on that.

JAMES: Okay … I won't say anything. Just make sure you know what you're doing. Devante is not going to wait forever—you already know that. It's just so messed up. Girl, get it together. Devante is a catch. I can't date him because he's my best friend. He's also not gay. (*He laughs.*) It's a shame, but I deal with it. I won't say anything to Devante. I promise.

That conversation was crazy. James understood for the most part, but I knew I needed to do something quick. That Monday I went to Mrs. Gandolfini's office to talk about my problem with Carlos. How many times was I going to talk to her? How many times was she going to tell me to make the right decision? Why was this so hard for me? Why did I still need Mrs. Gandolfini to tell me to break up with Carlos? She didn't actually tell me to break up with him, though; she usually put the ball in my court.

Well, I went to see her, and she didn't tell me anything new. She already knew what I needed to do, so it was just up to me. How many things could Mrs. Gandolfini tell me that I didn't know already? "It sounds like Devante means a lot to you," she said.

Yes, I told her about Devante. I can't remember if that was the first time I'd ever mentioned him, but I did say something about Devante and our feelings for each other. Of course she didn't agree with me dating two men. (Why do I keep calling them men? She didn't want me dating two guys.) I knew that I needed to make a decision. Mrs. Gandolfini knew what I needed to do, so it was just up to me to do it. I didn't know if I needed help doing it, but I knew it needed to be done soon. That meeting lasted an hour.

When I left Mrs. Gandolfini's office, Mercedes was walking down the hall. We were both on our way home, but Mercedes saw me and decided to stop and talk. She didn't talk about Carlos, surprisingly. Instead she started talking about Devante. Then she started talking about Carlos and Devante. Then she started talking about my brother. She was all over the place. Maybe she'd decided to avoid talking about Carlos and Devante, and so she brought up Anoki as a distraction. Mercedes was crafty; I could never read her mind.

We went to her house to do our homework and hang out. Luisa was there when we arrived, and Alicia came over a few minutes later. After we did our homework, we just sat in Mercedes's living room and talked. Of course I mentioned my conversation with Devante. Somehow Mercedes already knew about it. I was not surprised. She always knew something when it came to our crew.

"So what's new, Nita?" Luisa asked. "Is everything okay with Devante?"

"I knew that you would ask that sooner or later." I replied. "After all, Carlos is my boyfriend. Why can't you acknowledge that?"

When she said she asked because of what Mercedes had said to her, I realized that they had been discussing me and Devante.

"Devante and I had a conversation about how I was doing," I said. "Of course it was about Carlos."

Mercedes stared at me the whole time and then said, "Girl, you know it's much more than that. We want to know what you are doing with Carlos when Devante is your boo. You know it, I know it, everyone knows it."

I have to admit that I was laughing, because Mercedes said that so funny. I knew they weren't joking though, so I did give them an answer. "Devante and I are fine. He's just upset because I'm still with Carlos. Can you blame him? He loves me and I love him too. It's just difficult, that's all."

Alicia is always understanding, but I think by then she was as upset with me as everyone else in my life. She gave me a stern look, one I've never seen before, and said, "Nita, you know what to do. Do it please. Devante is a great guy. He's really nice. Carlos is not as nice as Devante. Do you need our help?"

Telling her that I didn't need their help, I calmly declined her offer. It was something I just needed to figure out for myself. I'm sure they understood, but I don't think they liked it.

CHAPTER 12

Where Do We Go from Here?

What was I doing? My guidance counselor, Mrs. Gandolfini, had helped me, but I didn't listen to her. My friends had tried to help me, but I didn't want to hear what they had to say. My family wanted to help, but I didn't want to listen to them either. Mrs. Gandolfini said that the ball was in my court. She was right.

That Saturday morning, my dad knocked on my bedroom door. I had it closed because, once again, I was crying. I think I felt stuck because of Carlos—although to be honest, it wasn't even Carlos's fault. It was all mine.

My dad had always been a strong father. He never made me feel like I could not go to him for something. I just thought that I needed to be strong for him; actually, he was strong for the whole family. I didn't have to be strong for him, and he made me see that I could always lean on him when I was hurting. We had a nice conversation that morning. This is how it went:

> DAD: How are you feeling, princess? Me and your mom are worried about you.

> ME: I'm fine, Dad. I just have a lot of things on my mind.

DAD: Is everything okay, sweetheart? Your mom said you had some troubles. I hope it's not about that boy. I know you haven't gotten rid of him yet. I don't want to ask you what's the matter, because I know you will tell me the truth.

ME: I don't know what's wrong with me, Daddy. Maybe I'm just crazy. I really liked Carlos, but I know he's not good for me. And I already know that you guys don't think he's good for me. Maybe he isn't. I know my friends want to help me, but it just feels like I need to do this by myself. I don't want to worry you, Daddy.

DAD: Come on … you're going to be fine. I've told you what to do already. The fact that you chose not to do it yet is on you. You always seem to do the right thing when your family is concerned. When you get it together, you will figure something out. We can't grow up for you. Your mom and I just want the best for our children. We won't tell you the wrong thing, and we won't steer you in the wrong direction. It's very simple:

Carlos is no good. Yes, he's doing good by his child, but how does he treat you? That's what you have to consider. It's not that he has a child, because we all make mistakes—not that the child was a mistake, but you understand what I'm saying. You will make the right decision. You know what to do, and I know you'll do it. I don't get why it's so hard for you to make a decision, but I'm sure you can see that now. Your mother and I won't worry you too much. If we see you're having a hard time though, we may have to make the decision for you.

Me: I know, Daddy. I know what to do.

What a conversation. My dad was one of the smartest men I knew. Actually, he *was* the smartest man I knew, and he still is. Men will come and go, guys will come and go, but my dad will always be my dad. Well, my dad said it best (he always did): I didn't know what Carlos was going through with his parents, but it wasn't my problem. Maybe I thought I could change him. (That's what females do. We always think we can change someone.) I don't know what I was thinking at the time. Carlos didn't think he needed to change, I guess because he didn't think he was hurting anyone. I never stopped to think that my family and friends were hurting as well.

Dating seemed so hard. Just when I thought I had the guy of my dreams, he turned out to be someone I needed to get away from. Carlos was a good guy underneath all the layers, but he wasn't my guy. I needed to subtract him from the equation and add no one. It took me a while to understand that. I didn't need to replace him with Devante; I just needed to take Carlos out of the picture altogether. If Devante decided to be with me, that was definitely a bonus.

Carlos was acting kind at the moment. I just didn't know how long he was going to stay that way. When Carlos and I were together, everything seemed to make sense to me, at least for that time, anyway. Love in high school is different than love in adulthood. Love in high school is premature: you don't really know what love is, and you can see everything you want right in front of your face. Adult love is more mature; you know what you want. As a teenager, I didn't know what I wanted, so Carlos just seemed like the best choice at the time.

It was Monday again. It always seemed to come so fast. Mercedes texted me: "Meet us after fifth period. Luisa and I have something to talk to you about really quickly."

What in the world could that crazy girl have to say right now? I hoped it had nothing to do with me. My friends had really given me grief about Carlos, and I didn't want to hear it. There had to be something else to talk about besides me and my relationship problems with Carlos.

Anyway, when fourth period came around, I buried my head in my book, waiting for fifth period to start. Lo and behold, Mercedes and Luisa found me in my class. (Okay, so I wasn't going to find them. I didn't want to know what they had to say, especially if it concerned me.) They came up to me smiling, and so I thought that maybe this didn't have anything to do with me.

Mercedes said, "I know you heard, girl. You know what happened to me right?"

Luisa smiled brightly. "Nita, why are you looking like you're surprised? Didn't you hear?"

I looked at them in amazement and said, "I really don't know what either of you are saying right now. What happened? Spill it!" Mercedes always had something crazy going, so I just humored her.

"Alan called me last night!"

Alan called her last night? Why was Alan calling any of my friends? Well, at least it wasn't about me. So I guessed I was happy for Mercedes.

We talked until fifth period started, and then my teacher told them they needed to go to class. After school, we met up at the pizza shop. Of course Carlos was in there with his boys, but I didn't let it get to me. Carlos saw me and smiled. Mercedes, Luisa, and I were talking about Alan and Mercedes hooking up. Of course, "hooking up" at that time just meant hanging out or getting together. It had nothing to do with sex. I had fun talking about Alan and Mercedes. I asked her what they talked about, and she just said they had a long conversation about the future. It sounded sincere, so I wanted to know everything she had to say. It was nice having a break from talking about Carlos and me.

I was glad I'd talked to Mercedes. Alan was a good guy, so I knew he would treat her right. Now, about Carlos and me ... At times he treated me right, but it wasn't an ongoing thing. It wasn't like my mom and dad or Orlana and her boyfriend. It wasn't even like Mercedes and Alan, although they were still a new couple. What was my relationship like, anyway? When my mom told me love was simple, I understood what she meant. She was saying that it doesn't take much to love someone, especially when they are doing right by you. Carlos was right sometimes, but he needed to be right all the time. Maybe he didn't know he needed to change, but I knew he needed to change.

A few days went by and it was already Thursday night. There was no class that Friday. (It had something to do with the teachers. I think they were cleaning up their files or something.) Anyway, Carlos came by to take me out to dinner. He seemed to always have money to do the things I liked to do. His mom wasn't on his back about me, because she knew I was legit. I wasn't out to get his money, so there was no reason for her to worry about me.

Carlos and I arrived at one of my favorite spots, Blue Moon, a famous seafood place on the South Side. Carlos was such a gentleman that night—I remember it so well. He was so nice to me that night that I didn't believe it was him. He treated me like my dad would treat my mom. Of course, I was feeling a little weird; Carlos was never nice like that. We talked the whole night, sitting by the window of the restaurant. The night was beautiful, so I didn't think there could be any problems. Was he trying to forget everything that happened between us? Was he delusional? Did he think that dinner going to make up for those times he hurt me? I didn't think so. I loved Carlos, but I was tired of the roller-coaster ride we were on. But at least that night I was able to put everything behind me. I didn't think about the hard times Carlos and I had when he mistreated me. I just thought about the good times. I kept thinking, *Carlos is such a nice guy. Maybe he's changed.* Had Carlos changed? I didn't think so. It was just nice to be with a guy who acted like he cared about me.

All that changed when we got in the car after our fabulous date. As Carlos was driving me home, he got a phone call from his mother, and so he pulled over to the side of the road to answer it. He was happy when he first answered the phone, but then his attitude changed when she told him something he didn't need to hear: Rhonda had called to say she was coming to take their daughter, Tinequa, back to the Dominican Republic to live with her and her family. Of course, Carlos was not appreciating that. He didn't know what he would do without his daughter, and he didn't even think Rhonda was a good mother. From what I'd heard,

Carlos was not a good guy for Rhonda. That's why she left him. I never got a chance to talk to Rhonda about it.

Now Carlos was furious. The drive home was silent. I wanted to say something, but I knew he had a temper. I didn't want to make him mad at me. Finally I just said, "I'm here for you, babe, for whatever you need." I thought maybe he could use some sympathy from me, since it seemed like his world was crumbling around him.

He didn't really want to hear that right then. When he pulled up in front of my house, he said, "I know you think you're helping me, but you're not. Rhonda probably wants to take my baby because of you. You're probably the reason she left. Just go in the house, please."

I didn't know what to say, so I just went inside. What happened? Carlos was being so nice to me, and now he was treating me like yesterday's garbage. Why did he talk to me like that? I didn't think I deserved any of that. I went to my room, sat down on the bed, and looked at the clock on my dresser. It was about eight o'clock. I didn't cry; I just stared at the wall in front of me. I hadn't closed the door. I think I wanted everyone to know that I was home. But no one came in my room that night. I guess they just wanted me to rest. Maybe I didn't need to talk that night. Maybe I just needed to be alone.

When I woke up that Tuesday morning, I felt numb all over. I went down to the kitchen for breakfast and found that everyone was at the table except my dad, who always left really early for work. Everyone was laughing, but I didn't feel like laughing that morning. While I was sitting at the table, I got a text message from Carlos: "Sorry for talking to you like that yesterday. Last night I wasn't myself because of what Rhonda said. Please forgive me."

We clearly needed to talk, but I wasn't sure if I wanted to talk with him. Rhonda hadn't come to take the baby yet, and I was afraid of what would happen when she did. Was I going to get hurt this time? Was Carlos going to yell at me again? I wasn't ready for the aftermath of that incident.

Anoki looked at me and said, "I know you're thinking about something. What is it?"

I didn't know what to tell him, because I knew he hated my situation with Carlos.

"I'm okay," I told him. "Don't worry about me."

He looked at me again and said, "I know you're okay. Just remember that we are here for you."

I knew my family was there for me. I guess that's what made everything worth trying. I knew if I tried new things, my family would always be there to support me.

We all left the table for school while my mom stayed behind to clean up our breakfast dishes.

As I was walking down the street away from my house, I couldn't help but wonder if there was something wrong with me. Maybe I was the crazy one for being in love. There were a few things to consider here: I went with the dude who was crazy gorgeous; I liked that he was Puerto Rican like me; he was kind and charming; he listened to me; and he had the most amazing eyes. Carlos was everything that I wanted in a guy—and just when I thought our relationship was going to be perfect, it ended up being a disaster. So I decided to continue to wait to break up with Carlos.

I thought about what I'd be losing if I stopped seeing him. I would be losing a guy who would always hold my hand and would walk me to class every day. In high school, that's everything. You always want someone to be with and spend the day with you. When you're in high school, the world is very different. When you're young you think you can live forever. In reality, however, things change very fast—I didn't know whether I was coming or going. I was very grateful to have parents, siblings, and great friends who understood me. It was too bad that I didn't understand myself. Maybe that's how it is when you're young.

I don't think we'll ever understand relationships. Relationships will always be there, and we'll never understand them. No one understands why guys and girls are different. No one understands why guys get mad and hit girls. It's never okay to do that, yet it happens all the time.

It took a lot of courage for me to figure out what to do about Carlos. He was wonderful at first; I guess that's why it was so hard for me to break up with him. I wondered what Mercedes would have done had she been the one dating him. Come on, she would've kicked his ass already. Sure … of course.

When I got home that Tuesday, I called Luisa. I had to use the house phone because my iPhone was broken. I dropped it, like I always do. Anyhow, I called Luisa to talk about Carlos. I knew she probably wouldn't want to hear what I had to say about the guy she couldn't stand. But she was my friend and a sister, so I figured, *Why not tell her?* When she answered the phone I said, "Luisa, you're home. I've been meaning to talk to you."

As Luisa was very nurturing, she said, "Hi, Nita. So what's going on, girl?"

I really hadn't wanted to call Luisa, but I didn't know what else to do. I couldn't have called Mercedes because she was such a crazy girl. I didn't feel like dealing with her because of her hatred for Carlos. I knew that Luisa wouldn't be biased, so I called her instead. This is how that conversation went:

> ME: I know you don't want to talk about this, but I need you.

> LUISA: I knew you would call at some point. This has to be about Carlos and the breakup. Maybe I should say the big breakup. Okay, girl, what's going on?

> ME: I need your help. I don't want to tell the crew that I'm breaking up with Carlos. I don't want to tell them when I'm going to break up, either. I'm telling you because it has to be said, and I have to make sure that I'm going to

do it. I'm definitely going to break up with Carlos—I've thought of so many reasons. Also, when we went out to dinner Tuesday night, his mom called and said that Rhonda was coming to pick up the baby. She's taking her back to the Dominican Republic.

LUISA: Wow! That is crazy, Nita. Rhonda is a trip. She is no good either. I don't know why she's taking the baby down. Why do they even live in in the Dominican Republic? Isn't that a poor country?

ME: I don't know, girl. Maybe they feel they can work it out, but I don't see how. Carlos seemed pretty mad, too. I didn't know what to say to him. I was trying to be caring, but he got angry.

LUISA: He didn't hit you, did he? If he did, we'll kill him.

ME: No, I'm okay. He just said some mean things. He said that maybe I'm the reason that Rhonda left. I was so hurt. I came home Tuesday night and just stared at the clock on my dresser. He just gets so angry. Carlos was never like that before. I didn't know what to think or do. Something must be done about this situation.

LUISA: Nita, we are always here for you. If you want me just to be here right now, I'll do that instead. So what do you need from me?

ME: I don't really need anything. I just need you to know how I feel and what happened. I can't tell Mercedes because you know how she is. I can't tell Alicia because you know how she is. I can't tell Anoki or Orlana because they'll tell my parents. I can't tell Alan because I don't want to worry him.

LUISA: Okay, I won't tell anyone. I just want you to be safe; we all do. Carlos is not good for you. You've learned that, but you can end it. Like I said, we are here for you. Do you want us there when you do it?

ME: No, I need to do it. I know you want to help, but I really need to do this by myself. Carlos is a hard enough job for me—I don't want to put anyone

through this. I can handle him. Don't
worry about it. Please don't tell any of
our crew or anyone in my family. I got
this.

It was hard to tell Luisa that I didn't need their help. I'm
glad she knew what I meant, and understood. I liked it when
my friends cared about me. My family loved me too, so I
didn't have to worry about anything. The only hard part now
was to find the best time to talk to Carlos.

After I got off the phone with Luisa, I went into my
room to do my homework and Orlana knocked on the door.
She said, "I was just thinking about you. How's everything
going?"

I told her the truth: I was fine, but I was having trouble
with Carlos.

She said she'd heard me talking on the phone. "So you're
going to break up with Carlos this time? Okay, so I'm sure
you have a plan. From what I heard, you sound sure of this
plan. I don't want to tell you anything, because I'm sure you
have an idea what you want to do. Just know that Carlos is
a schemer, so he'll do anything to keep you, or he'll try at
least. You see that for yourself. You know how he is."

I pulled Orlana into my room and closed the door, and
we talked about my plan for breaking up with Carlos. I
felt good about the plan, because I wasn't including anyone
but myself and Carlos. I told Orlana that I wanted Luisa to
know, but not the whole crew. I didn't want Mom or Dad or
Anoki to know. She understood, but I know she wanted to

help. She went back to her room, wishing me good luck and promising not to tell the family. Orlana was always good at keeping secrets in the house when it came to me. Anoki, on the other hand, told everything he heard in the house. No secrets with him.

Thursday morning I woke up at seven and got ready in a hurry. I went downstairs, ate breakfast with the family, and met Mercedes, Luisa, and Alicia at the corner by my house. I didn't wait for Carlos to call me or come by. I didn't really want to deal with him that day. Part of me missed him, and part of me didn't care much.

Mercedes couldn't help but tell me, "I know what's going on, Nita. It's okay though. We understand, and we won't interfere. You know me though. If he hits you, he's going down." I listened to Mercedes and thanked her. Alicia put her arm around me and just kept it there. I knew what she was saying.

School was easy that day. After first period, I went to talk to Mrs. Gandolfini. I knew she'd want to hear from me, since we haven't spoken in a long time. I wanted to tell her that I'd finally decided to break up with Carlos—I didn't know what day yet, but I wasn't including my family and all my friends.

Mrs. Gandolfini didn't look up when I came into her office, but I sat down anyway. When she did see me, she said, "I knew you'd be in here one of these days. How is everything going? I haven't seen you in a while. I was hoping I would see you. How's the Carlos situation?"

I told her not to worry about me because I had it under control, and she said she understood why I didn't want to include everybody in the breakup. She said that I needed to take a stand by myself, that it would make me a better young lady. That's really all the motivation that I needed to break up with Carlos. I just didn't know when I was going to do it. I thought about doing it that day, but I wasn't sure. I thought about the weekend, but I wasn't sure about that either.

When I got home that day, I had an idea. I thought that maybe I should ask Carlos to come to my house. But I wasn't sure what my parents would say, so I didn't do that. I decided to just meet him in the park across the street from my house. After I did my homework, I called Carlos and asked him to come to the park and meet me. Then I went across the street to the park to wait. I wrote in my journal, and when I was done I looked up and saw Carlos coming across the street.

Mercedes texted me: "I just want you to know that I am thinking about you and so is the rest of the crew." I didn't answer, but I was happy to see that message, which gave me more motivation to do what I had to do. I knew it had been a long time coming, but at least I had it in my heart to do this one thing. I know all of you want to know what I said, so here is how it went:

ME: Hi, Carlos. How are you?

CARLOS: How's it going, babe? What's been going on?

ME: I wanted to talk to you. (*I feel a twinge of fear.*) It's time that we talk about us.

CARLOS: What's the problem, babe? Is everything okay?

ME: Not really. (*Here's where it gets weird.*) Carlos, I am tired of your mood swings. You get mad and then you take it out on me. I don't know what to do anymore. You don't give me any choice. Every time I have a comment, you get angry. That's no way for a relationship to go. I know we're young and in love, but there has to be more for me. You're not ready for a relationship, and maybe I'm not either.

CARLOS: I can't believe you're telling me this. (*This is where Carlos gets angry.*) What are you talking about? We have a great relationship. What is your problem? You always do this! What do you want from me? (*This is where he slowly calms down.*) Okay, I'm sorry I yelled, but you have to understand—Rhonda

is taking my daughter, and now you're
acting this way.

ME: I never meant to hurt you, Carlos, but
we need to … break up.

CARLOS: What?

Before you guys start worrying, Carlos did not hit me.
He did not push me or get angrier. I know that's not the
norm, but that's what happened. Now that you know what
happened, I can continue the story:

ME: I'm sorry, Carlos, but you know the
problems we face. I'm not happy,
and you have too many problems to
be so young. I'm not happy in this
relationship. You change too much. I
know you have a lot going on in your
life, but it's not fair. I wish things could
have worked out, but we have to end
this relationship. I know you're angry—
that's no surprise. Being a father should
make you more understanding. I don't
parents. Maybe I don't have to. Once
again, I am sorry about this, but we
have to end this relationship now, before
anyone gets hurt. So maybe we'll see
each other in school.

> CARLOS: Wow! Well, if that's what you want. I do love you, so ... I guess I have to let you go. (*Tears actually welled up in his eyes.*)

> ME: I love you too, Carlos. Just know that I still care about you. We can be friends, or we can do whatever you want. We just can't be together as a couple.

> CARLOS: Okay, that's fair.

Just like that, it was over. Yeah, I know—that was simple. What about those relationships that don't end so nicely? What if Carlos had hit me? At the end of the day, Carlos still had anger problems. I was just glad that he didn't take them out on me. It didn't matter if Carlos wanted to stay with me; I knew I needed to get out.

What about those people who don't get out of abusive relationships? Well, hopefully they have family and friends who can help them along the way. I have to admit it wasn't easy breaking up with Carlos, because everyone knew I loved him. But I also knew that I needed to get out.

At the end of our conversation, Carlos gave me a warm hug. I'd never felt a hug like that from him. Had I changed him? I don't know the answer to that, and I don't think I'll ever know. But I'm glad it ended the way it did.

When I finally said goodbye to Carlos, I was a little sad, to be honest. I also knew that my love for him was real. I knew that I would never forget him. After all, he was my first true love. It may have not been the most perfect relationship, but it was real.

While I was walking back to my house across the street from the park, Carlos called out, "Nita, take care of yourself!"

I want to cry, but I just said, "You take care of yourself too, Carlos." At first I wondered why Carlos didn't walk me to my house, but then later that night I realized that when I said it was over, he must have gotten the message and decided to just let it go. That was smart, I guess.

When I got inside the house, I shed a tear. Then I texted Mercedes and said, "I did it girl!" She texted me back, "The crew and I are coming over now." The crew was crazy, but they meant well, as always.

Anoki was at home, cooking something on the stove. He looked at me with his crazy smile and said, "Are you okay, Sis?"

I looked at him and sat down. "Yeah, Bro. I did it. I broke up with Carlos, finally."

For a moment he was speechless. He took his food off the stove and sat down across from me to eat. "Whoa!" he said. "How are you feeling?"

I assured him that I was okay. He had always been a loving brother, so I was glad to talk to him about my breakup with Carlos. Then Orlana came into the kitchen and said, "I think you guys are talking about something important. What is it?"

Anoki couldn't help himself. "I knew she would do it," he said. "Nita broke up with Carlos. Good! I hate his dumb ass."

Orlana was in a state of shock. She didn't know what to say. All she could do was sit down next to me and give me a hug around my shoulders.

After talking with my family, I heard a knock on the door. It was my crew, of course. I let them in, and we sat in the living room. James was the first to speak. "I just want to congratulate you, girl. This took so long for you to do. It must feel good." James had a different view of my relationship, so I got where he was coming from.

Mercedes looked at me and said, "Nita, you are our girl. We wanted to be there, but I guess you had your reasons for doing it alone. We love you and always will." Luisa already knew what I was going to do, so she just sat there on the couch. Alicia gave me a hug, as usual. We talked until nighttime.

My friends and family were there for me, and I was very lucky. Mercedes couldn't help herself that night when she said, "Now that Carlos is gone, what about Devante?"

I'd almost forgotten about Devante. I was so caught up in breaking up with Carlos that I'd totally forgotten that I wanted to be with Devante. Then I began wondering if I even deserved Devante. He needed somebody without drama. I guess when I lost Carlos, I lost the drama. At the time I was really confused, but of course Mercedes and the crew got me back into shape.

After my friends left, around eight thirty, I texted Devante. "Hey Devante. I just want you to know that I am … a free girl."

He texted me back. "Wow … I'm happy for you. Are you doing okay?"

"I'm fine."

We texted until ten, and then I realized it was time to go to bed.

Texting with him was wonderful. I didn't want to call him because I didn't want to pressure him into anything that he might not have wanted to do at the time. If this relationship with Carlos had taught me anything, it was that patience is very important. I hadn't taken the time to find out some important details about Carlos before dating him. I learned that it was smart to get to know a guy before starting a relationship with him. Carlos was cool, but I learned that I needed more than just a cool guy; I needed an understanding guy, and I needed a guy who didn't have anger problems.

Friday came, and I was ready to face the music. The crew was coming to pick me up from my house, and while I was waiting for them in the living room, my parents came downstairs and said simultaneously, "We knew you could do it."

My mom said, "I love you Nita."

My dad just smiled his biggest smile. I guess that's how he communicated something that he couldn't explain.

After I'd chatted with my parents for a minute or two, my crew showed up at the door. I walked to school with them, and I felt so happy. I was happy because I was free. I was happy because I'd let Carlos go. Again, Carlos wasn't a bad guy. He was just in a bad place for being so young.

Going to school felt normal that day. After classes were over, I stopped by Mrs. Gandolfini's office and said, "I'm free." She knew what I meant by that, and she gave me a big hug. She was also speechless, like Orlana. We talked for about five minutes in her office. She always inspired me. Mrs. Gandolfini was one of those guidance counselors you never forget. She was an awesome woman.

As my crew and I were going home, we stopped by the pizza shop near the school. Sitting in a booth at the pizza shop was someone I had been thinking about all day: Devante. The crew had lured me there so I could see him. Mercedes looked at me with her crazy look, as always, and said, "I hope you guys have fun. Good-bye, Nita and Devante." Luisa and Alicia looked at each other and then looked at me. Then they said together, "Bye, you guys. Have fun …"

That was so sneaky, but I didn't mind. Devante had been on my mind, so I'm guessing James put Devante up to it.

Well, we stayed in the pizza shop until it was time to go home—around ten o'clock, since it was a Friday night. Devante and I talked for hours after school that day. Carlos was just a memory; I didn't have to worry about that anymore. I did appreciate what we had, though. I'd learned to love him, so that made me ready to want to be with another guy. Devante and I talked all night, but we didn't make plans for the future. We just enjoyed each other's company.

When it was time to go home, Devante drove me home in his BMW, and while he was walking me to my door, he gave me a kiss on the cheek. Then he said, "I'll call you tomorrow. Have a good night." That was a perfect ending to a beautiful day with Devante.

Printed in the United States
By Bookmasters